'Aw, Kate.

'How am I ever going ~~~~~~~~~~ you if you keep running away?'

Kate was silent. Sam fell into step beside her.

'I'm the new boy at school,' he said plaintively. 'I need to make some friends.'

'Why pick on me?' Kate responded. 'You've already made friends with half the hospital.' She threw Sam a curious glance as they made their way through the gates. 'Are they all like you in Australia?'

'Nope. I'm one of a kind.'

'Thank God for that.'

'I may have met an awful lot of people since I came here,' Sam told her, 'but it's you I'm really interested in, Katy.'

Alison Roberts was born in New Zealand and, she says, 'I lived in London and Washington DC as a child and began my working career as a primary-school teacher. A lifelong interest in medicine was fostered by my doctor and nurse parents, flatting with doctors and physiotherapists on leaving home, and marriage to a house surgeon who is now a consultant cardiologist. I have also worked as a cardiology technician and research assistant. My husband's medical career took us to Glasgow for two years, which was an ideal place and time to start my writing career. I now live in Christchurch, New Zealand, with my husband, daughter and various pets.'

Recent titles by the same author:

MUM'S THE WORD
A CHANCE IN A MILLION

ONE OF
A KIND

BY
ALISON ROBERTS

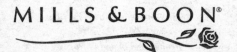

MILLS & BOON®

First published in Great Britain 1999
Harlequin Mills & Boon Limited,
Eton House, 18-24 Paradise Road, Richmond, Surrey TW9 1SR

© Alison Roberts 1999

ISBN 0 263 81678 8

Set in Times Roman 10½ on 12 pt.
03-9905-45769-D

Printed and bound in Norway
by AIT Trondheim AS, Trondheim

CHAPTER ONE

THE sense of the unfamiliar presence in the room was overpowering.

Kate Campbell swung to confront the intruder, protective of her jurisdiction and annoyed at the disturbance of her meticulous and urgent routine. Her verbal challenge was forgotten momentarily, however, and her eyes widened at the extraordinary sight before her.

The man was enormous. Six feet four if he was an inch, Kate registered, and broad-shouldered as well. He looked like a bear. It was not simply his size that was so startling. His tousled mop of blond curls was streaked almost white in places and his face was bronzed to the point of making his teeth look unnaturally white. Kate had to dismiss the impression of a toothpaste commercial.

She was distantly aware that in the midst of the depressing climb out of another London winter it was really not acceptable to see someone who looked as though he had never lived in anything but blazing sunshine. And those teeth! She could see almost every single one in the wide grin that was being directed at her. The thought that the man looked like a muppet flashed through Kate's critical mind.

The grin changed shape even as she was aware of her initial impressions.

'G'day!'

The accent was as out of place as the tan. Kate

heard the sharp intake of breath beside her as her junior colleague turned at the sound. Kate's eyes narrowed again as she realised that the control of her domain had slipped another notch. Margo was inclined to be distracted by any good-looking males who were at least conscious. Kate hated to think of the effect on the girl's concentration that would ensue from the sight of this specimen, lounging against the wall.

Lounging! Kate felt the stirrings of outrage. An elbow had displaced two boxes of surgical gloves and the hip propped on the bench-top had disrupted the line of carefully sorted needle-boxes arranged according to gauge. Kate's intake of breath was also sharp but for reasons very different to Margo's.

'Finish checking that suction equipment and test the defibrillators,' she ordered the junior nurse tersely. Her gaze flicked back to the huge stranger.

'Just who the hell are you?' she snapped.

The wide grin was back in a flash. 'S.A. Marshall. But call me Sam.' A hand was extended—an oversized paw with a smattering of fine, bleached hair, the skin even browner than his face.

Kate ignored the gesture. 'Do you have any idea where you are?'

'I'm kind of hoping I'm in the emergency department of St Matthew's Hospital.' Clear blue eyes regarded Kate steadily and she could swear they were twinkling with amusement.

'To be a little more precise,' Kate informed him acidly, 'you are in a resuscitation area, used to treat critically ill people, some of whom are expected shortly from a major vehicle accident. A place you have no right to be.'

Kate moved purposefully towards the man, hoping to brush him aside as she reached for the bench. At the last possible moment he straightened, allowing Kate to begin pointedly to rearrange the needle boxes. When he moved no further away Kate turned her head to glare at him.

'If you need medical attention I suggest you go to the front desk. It may not be the usual procedure where you come from but I can assure you it is here. If necessary I can alert Security.'

'Do you have a name or shall I just call you "Boss"?'

The giggle from Margo was accompanied by a shake of her red curls and an admiring smile, but the effort gained her nothing more than a transfer of Kate's disapproving glare. The girl turned back hurriedly to the equipment she was checking.

Kate turned back to the intruder very slowly. For the first time in many years she was unsure of how to handle the situation in which she found herself. Her confusion was infuriating, which only exacerbated the problem. When the swing doors to the resuscitation area bumped open to admit the junior emergency department consultant, Julian Calder, she was relieved and almost pleased. Almost.

'There you are, Sam. Sorry about that. Call of nature, you understand.'

Kate certainly understood. She could bet that the call of nature had been the new student nurse she had left, observing, in the reception area. She nodded at the consultant who was now gazing appreciatively at Margo's legs as she reached for an item on a high shelf.

'Are you aware that we have a multiple RTA on the way?' Kate asked. 'Up to eight casualties but at least two are trapped and may take some time.'

Julian's expression was relaxed. 'Fun and games.' He turned to the man beside him. 'Good introduction for you, Sam. Do you want to watch or shall we throw you a pair of gloves?'

Kate's confusion escalated as she observed the change in demeanour of the huge man. Without any obvious movement she could sense the collection and new focus of concentration. It simply didn't fit. The man was wearing jeans and a faded denim shirt, which was largely unbuttoned over a tight-fitting white T-shirt. That he would be of any use in an emergency medical situation seemed as unlikely as him having acquired his tan on a recent trip to Brighton. Sam's response to the invitation was pre-empted by the swing doors, opening to admit a male nurse.

'Kate? About eight minutes. Two status 3s on the way. One's got multiple trauma, including a mid-shaft compound fracture of the right femur—possibly KOed. The other's sustained major chest injuries. There are two children coming in as well—status 1. Two more are being freed from a vehicle—status unknown.'

Kate nodded. Status 3 meant the victims were in a dangerous condition—unstable and could die at any time. At least the children weren't badly injured.

'Thanks, Joe. Better warn Reception to bump up the waiting time. Anyone who can go to their GPs would be well advised to do so. Make it another two hours at least.'

Kate's glance was scanning the resuscitation area as she spoke. They were as ready as they could ever be. Luckily the day had been relatively quiet so far and the last occupants of the four-bed resus. area were stable enough to go to Theatre and the wards as soon as word of the incoming RTA was received.

The swing doors were in constant motion now as staff gathered. The atmosphere was deceptively relaxed as they greeted each other and chatted. Kate knew the tension would kick in the instant the first ambulance arrived. She reached for a fresh pair of gloves and found herself crowded as the senior emergency department consultant, Jeff Merrick, and two senior registrars arrived and requested gowns and gloves. Jeff nodded over Kate's shoulder to acknowledge Sam.

'I didn't think you were starting until tomorrow.'

'Julian's been giving me a tour. I may be in the way now, though.'

'Nonsense. We could use the help. Kate here will find you some gear.' He turned to Kate. 'Have you been introduced to Dr Marshall?'

'Not exactly,' Kate said cautiously. The name now struck a chord that had been wiped from her memory by having been thrown off balance by the earlier intrusion. She avoided Dr Marshall's eye, glancing instead at those huge paws. Even the largest size surgical gloves might be inadequate but she offered him the box anyway.

'Kate's our most experienced emergency nurse,' Jeff Merrick stated. 'We couldn't manage without her. Her instincts can be trusted at all times.'

Kate dropped her eyes at the unexpected praise. She covered her embarrassment by reaching for a sterilised pack, containing the largest size of gown, and ripped it open.

'Joe's another mainstay in the nursing team but Kate keeps our junior doctors in line. Even some not so junior,' Jeff added musingly. His gaze flicked over to where Julian was engaged in conversation with Margo, and Kate thought she detected a small sigh. She reached up to tie the top strings of Sam's gown.

'Sam's here from Sydney, Australia.' Jeff continued his introduction hurriedly. 'He's after some advanced training in emergency medicine for six months, though I can't fathom why—given his experience and reputation already.'

Kate's modesty at the praise of her own abilities was clearly not shared by S.A. Marshall, though his grin was a little one-sided. 'No one's ever experienced enough. Your throughput in a month is probably more than I'd see in six months back home. Emergency work under pressure is what I'm after.'

'You're about to get it.' Kate handed him a lead apron—a necessary precaution for all staff members because of the number of X-rays which were taken in the department, though disliked for their cumbersome weight. She showed him how to fasten it as the first stretcher was wheeled in. It was closely followed by a second and two wailing children with cervical collars, being carried by paramedic staff.

Pandemonium replaced the earlier expectant calm as staff transferred the seriously injured adults to the beds and gained as much information as possible from the ambulance crews. The two children went to the third bed in the area with a junior registrar and two nurses, quickly screened by the side curtains. Kate nodded to Joe who was at bed two with the chest injury and a team of juniors under the direction of Jeff Merrick and another registrar. She quickly moved their trolleys—with the equipment to establish airway control and IV access—closer and then whisked the curtain closed between them as her patient was transferred to bed one.

The patient, a forty-three-year-old male, was breathing on his own without difficulty at present so Julian moved to establish IV access, leaving a junior registrar to monitor the airway. Kate kept an eye on the nurses, applying ECG electrodes and a blood-pressure cuff, as she cut away the remainder of the man's clothing. Lying on his left side, the gross deformity and trauma to his right leg was only too obvious. Because of his position a junior nurse was having trouble positioning the ECG electrodes correctly.

Kate reached over to reposition them quickly, before handing Julian the IV cannula and syringes he required for drawing blood. She kept an eye on the monitors even as she reached for the test tubes to transfer the syringe full of blood that Julian thrust towards her.

'Type and crossmatch. Stat,' he added unnecessarily. Kate was well aware how severe the haemorrhage could be from an injury to the femoral shaft, and it was unlikely to be the only serious injury sustained. It took only seconds to label and pack the tubes into the cannister for the vacuum tube system and to punch the numbers for the blood bank into the keypad, before launching the samples. She heard Julian ordering more pain relief and drew up the drugs required, then paused for a moment to put her face close to the patient's.

'You're doing really well, John.' Kate listened to the muffled response from beneath the oxygen mask and nodded. 'I know. You've got a nasty broken leg. We're giving you something for the pain now.'

The noise level in the resuscitation area was increasing. Jeff Merrick was struggling with the chest injury case, who was deteriorating. An anaesthetist had taken over airway control but an arrest seemed imminent and orders were being shouted to be heard over the general hubbub. The small children were still screaming and Kate was relieved to see one being carried from the area. It was no place for them if it could be avoided.

To a casual observer the area was like bedlam, but Kate's practised eye could see that things were running as smoothly as possible. Staff numbers were good. Major problems would occur if serious new cases arrived too soon, however, and Kate's level of alertness was high. Even through the general noise level and her own level of concentration she found herself acutely aware of the medical newcomer's voice, the deepness and unusual accent cutting through the background volume.

'Traction splint before X-ray?' he was suggesting.

Julian nodded his agreement. 'Reduction in pain and associated haemorrhage is fairly well documented now. Kate?'

Kate was already moving, annoyed that she hadn't thought to have the splint there already. She would have if her set-up routine hadn't been disrupted. She moved in as the registrar spoke to the patient.

'John? We're going to straighten your leg a bit.

It'll hurt like hell but will start feeling a lot better after that. OK?'

Kate saw the grim nod and moved to take hold of the man's hand. 'Squeeze as hard as you like,' she told him. 'We don't mind a bit of swearing, either.'

She had to grit her teeth against the pressure on her hand but the fortunately rapid procedure was endured in silence. As the X-ray technicians moved in with their bulky equipment Kate was aware that the frantic activity around the next bed signalled the cardiac arrest of Jeff Merrick's patient. She listened tensely to the efforts at resuscitation as she stood aside to allow X-ray access to John, breathing a sigh of relief when a normal rhythm was re-established. The relief was short lived, however, as she knew that Jeff now had a race against time to get his patient stabilised enough to get to Theatre. She was more dismayed to see the swing doors open to admit a new influx of paramedic staff and another stretcher.

Reaching for the replacement bag of IV fluid John required, Kate watched as Sam moved immediately to intercept the stretcher and take over the ambu bag as the new patient was rushed to the area now empty of children. She was aware of a pang of disappointment when Jeff Merrick deployed two other nurses to assist Sam but was relieved to allow her attention to be drawn elsewhere. Her instincts told her that the situation was well controlled and she had more than enough to think about, without having to monitor the actions of the blond giant who had entered her orbit so abruptly.

It was inevitable that the aftermath of a prolonged high-tension situation generated an excited camaraderie amongst the staff involved, and Kate wasn't surprised at the level of chatter and laughter as she returned to the resus. area, having accompanied John to Theatre. A massive clean-up was under way and Kate entertained the hope that things would remain quiet. At least the emergencies had had the positive effect of largely clearing the waiting room of minor cases.

Kate began to sort the debris on the nearest trolley, carefully picking out the needles to post into the sharps disposal container. Margo and another junior nurse came towards her, carrying a pile of bloody drapes for the linen sack. They had been assisting Sam, and Kate's attention was drawn back sharply to the stranger.

'How did it go?' she queried.

'Unbelievable!' Margo's green eyes were shining. 'There was no anaesthetist available and I've never seen anyone do a crash intubation so easily.'

Kate raised an eyebrow. It was a procedure that needed considerable experience and skill and one which was not undertaken lightly.

'She was practically dead,' Christine confirmed. 'So hypovolaemic I didn't think we had a chance. Ruptured spleen and she'd been trapped in the car for ages. She was the mother of those children that came in with the first load,' she added.

'Sam had her stabilised and into Theatre within thirty minutes,' Margo breathed.

Her blatant admiration irked Kate. She caught Joe's eye as he hurried past with an armload of IV fluid bags to restock the shelves.

'I must see if there's a white charger tied up in the ambulance bay,' he murmured.

'More likely to be a kangaroo,' Kate muttered. She caught the glance that passed between the junior nurses and was irritated anew at the effect Dr Marshall had had on all the staff—herself included. She raised her voice slightly. 'I imagine he's got one of those hats as well, with all the corks bobbing around the edge.'

The sudden silence that greeted her uncharacteristic comment made Kate look up as she collected the last of the plastic packaging from the trolley. She found herself looking into the blue eyes of Margo's new hero.

'I cut the corks off, actually,' he informed her with a wide grin. 'Bit passé.'

Kate refused to be embarrassed. It was bad enough for him to know she had been thinking about him, let alone gossiping like any other star-struck junior. But she could handle it. And why should she care what he thought, anyway? She was spared having to think up a suitable reply by the arrival of Julian, who dropped his lead apron casually onto the bed from where it promptly slid to the floor.

'Your spleen's just come out of Theatre,' he told Sam. 'She's doing fine.'

Kate saw undisguised pleasure light the features of the Australian but turned away. It was more likely pride in his own abilities than any empathy with the patient or her relatives. She suppressed her familiar irritation with the way Julian always referred to cases as parts of the body. She hated his apparent lack of empathy with the people they dealt with. Kate sent Margo to collect and clean the lead aprons and another nurse to retest and sort the suction equipment. She still overheard Sam's query, however.

'What's happened to the children?'

'I've no idea.' Julian was offhand. He stripped off his theatre gown, rolled it into a ball and thrust it towards Kate who accepted it automatically. 'They weren't badly injured.'

'But who's looking after them?' Sam persisted.

Kate shoved the gown into the linen bag as Julian shrugged.

'Social Services are caring for them at present,' Kate informed Sam. 'The grandparents are on their way.'

Sam nodded, satisfied. Kate had the absurd impression that if the answer hadn't been satisfactory he would have stormed off himself, intent on baby-sitting. She watched as Sam stripped off his own bloodied gown and rolled it up, holding out her hand in readiness.

Sam flicked her a glance but moved deliberately to deposit the bundle into the linen bag himself. Then he looked up and surprised her with a wink.

'I'm almost house-trained,' he said softly.

Kate's gaze shifted to Julian, wondering if he'd noticed the subtle criticism. Of course he hadn't.

'My leg's still in Theatre,' he was saying. 'There was a bit more to patch up than we'd realised.'

'I'm not surprised,' Sam replied. 'Did you know it takes about eight hundred kilograms of force to produce a mid-shaft fracture like that? Inevitable that it does some other damage along the way.'

Kate squeezed the last drapes into the now over-flowing linen bag and edged its wheeled frame past an abandoned oxygen tank. Julian yawned and moved towards the doors.

'I guess. At least my shift's nearly finished. I was

going to include one of our local watering holes in the tour if you fancy it. They might even come up with a cold beer if you're lucky.'

Sam was watching Kate manoeuvre the linen bag. 'Sounds good to me. What are you doing after work, Kate?'

Kate only just prevented her mouth from gaping in astonishment at the open invitation. Her gaze flew up to meet his but Julian's response was swift.

'You're wasting your time there, old chap. Know what I mean?' He gave Sam a knowing look and then shoved the swing door open. 'Now, let me introduce you to Margo.'

Julian was already moving purposefully through the department as Sam paused to hold the door open for Kate.

'You didn't answer my question,' he said quietly.

'I think Julian made things pretty clear,' Kate replied calmly. 'I'm sure you know what he meant.'

'I'm sure I did,' Sam agreed seriously. He was leaning against the swing door in such a position that Kate couldn't navigate the awkward linen bag, without opening the second door. She eyed him cautiously as he continued to block her way. If he was expecting a response to that statement he would be disappointed. But it was Sam who spoke next.

'I think,' he whispered, leaning towards Kate, 'that Julian meant you don't fancy him as much as he fancies himself.'

Kate couldn't help herself. She laughed. Behind Sam she could see Julian, returning with Margo in tow. The expressions on the faces of her colleagues was enough to kill her laughter instantly.

'Excuse me. I've got a lot to do.' Sam was forced

to step back hurriedly as Kate propelled her burden forward forcefully. She didn't look back.

The shower cubicle was a little offset to the main locker room so that unless the water was running it was not immediately obvious that the facility was in use. Kate had often overheard junior staff, making comments about her as she towelled off and changed. Today was no exception.

'I tell you, she was flirting.'

'She wouldn't have a clue how.'

'He made her laugh.'

'Never! She doesn't know how to do that either.'

Kate caught a glimpse of her reflection as she collected her underwear from the hook. She was as surprised as they were. Nobody made Kate Campbell laugh. Smile, yes—occasionally—but not laugh with the genuine amusement she had clearly felt. Even now the memory made her smile but she was puzzled, too. And a little disturbed. For someone who had rolled in like some human tidal wave Dr S.A. Marshall was rather too astute. Could Joe have said something?

No. Kate shook her head as she thrust a slim leg into the baggy grey trackpants. Joe would never betray a confidence and certainly not to a stranger. And Joe was the only one in the department who knew how Julian had pursued her and how her lack of interest had infuriated the young consultant. Joe hadn't witnessed the unpleasant physical struggle in the office when Julian had cornered her late one night, but he had heard the nasty verbal exchange that had followed and now had every sympathy with the tension and strained professional relationship Kate was experiencing.

Of course, there was one other person who knew about it, but the thought that Julian's version of events might have come up in conversation with the newcomer was too awful to contemplate.

The banging of locker doors advertised another arrival in the adjoining room. She recognised the voice as belonging to Jude, a good friend of Margo's.

'God, I'm late!'

'You're lucky Kate's not on.'

'Am I ever. Hi, Margo. Anything exciting happening?'

'How about a gorgeous single Australian who cruised in on his surfboard for six months advanced training? Starts tomorrow, officially.'

'What specialty?'

'Just emergency.' Margo was obviously delighted to have the information. 'He wants hands-on experience with difficult cases in all areas. Apparently, the other consultants have agreed to let him take on things they would normally be called in for—under supervision, of course.'

'Why? That's pretty unusual.'

'You won't believe it.' Margo sounded excited. 'He's got a post lined up with the Royal Australian Flying Doctor Service when he's finished here. He said they're often in a position of being out in the wilds, thousands of miles from anywhere, with a serious injury to deal with on their own. Sam says even observation is better than reading up techniques in a textbook, but he's hoping to get hands-on for as wide a variety of cases as possible.'

'You seem to have got to know a lot about him

rather quickly.' Jude sounded put out. 'Damn. I've lost a button.'

'Well, I overheard Jeff Merrick talking to the head of the orthopaedic department, actually,' Margo admitted. 'But I almost went out for a drink with him.'

'Oh?' Jude was unimpressed. 'Anyone got a safety pin?'

Kate finished lacing up her trainers and reached for her heavy, over-sized pullover. It all fitted with the rather over-the-top impression, she decided. A blond, sun-bronzed superhero, flying through deserted terrain to single-handedly save a life here or there.

Dangerous, she concluded, but she was unsure whether she was referring to the proposed career or the man himself. Joe would be amused to learn that the nineties equivalent of a white charger was probably a twin-engined Cessna. Rather against her will she tuned in to the nearby voices again.

'What did you say his name was?'

'Just Sam.'

'What, no surname?'

'He goes by his initials.' Margo giggled. 'S.A.M. M for Marshall, but he says to just call him Sam. I don't know what the S stands for.'

'I'm sure you'll find out.' Jude sounded weary. 'God, I hate my hair. What on earth am I going to do with it?'

'Shave it off,' a third voice suggested. 'Like Kate.'

There was a general wave of laughter and Kate stuffed her towel into her bag with some vigour. She turned to the mirror and fluffed her light brown hair with her fingers. OK, so it was short. Really short. It she let it grow more than the inch or so it had in length now it would start to curl. She could have a gorgeous tumble of tresses exactly like Margo if she wanted to, but she had no desire to do so. She liked the sleek, uncompromising image it gave her. It went with the fact that she never wore any make-up.

No-nonsense Kate. Competent, dedicated and quite sure of who she was and where she was going. Maybe it did cut her off from the crowd, made her seem different enough to be intimidating and unwelcome, but that was fine. In fact, that was exactly the way Kate wanted it.

She decided to make her exit from the shower cubicle in time to let the juniors know she had overheard their gossip but she dropped her locker key. As she bent to retrieve it she could hear the sounds of a mass exit and the girls saying their farewells to each other. She caught Jude's voice again.

'I can't wait to meet him. How old is he?'

'Too old for you. I heard Jeff say he was thirty-seven but he doesn't look it.'

'He's probably married.'

'He's not wearing a ring—and he's in single hospital accommodation.'

'Doesn't mean anything, but I won't let it put me off. Is he going to do nights?'

'I should think so. But you'll have some competition. He's got his eye on Kate.'

There was another shout of laughter, this time much fainter.

'What on earth would he see in *her*?'

'Beats me. Now, ask me what she might see in *him*...'

The locker room was empty as Kate pulled on her oilskin and jammed a woollen cap over her cropped hair. She turned to leave and face the journey home through the wintry evening but was caught by the sight of herself in another mirror.

What would he see in her, indeed? Large hazel eyes framed by a pale, elfin face stared back at her and Kate frowned. Looking so much younger than her twenty-eight years was no advantage to her image. She shrugged. It didn't matter. The cool aloofness that went with her professional abilities gave her all the authority she needed. Kate turned away from the mirror. There was nothing there to attract Dr S.A. Marshall—thank goodness.

Was there anything to attract her? Of course there was. Plenty. Nothing that she couldn't deal with and dismiss, however. Except…except that impression that he was somehow tuned in. That he might understand her more than anyone else had ever tried—or wanted—to.

Kate set off towards the bus stop. The headlights of the heavy traffic sent beams of light through the drizzle. The noise of the rush hour was a good distraction to an unwelcome train of thought. What did it matter what level of understanding the stranger was capable of? He wouldn't get the chance to find out about Kate. Nobody would. Not even Joe. Her secret was something she firmly intended to take to her grave with her. To share it might destroy her, and Kate had worked too long and too hard on herself to let that happen.

The arrival of a foreign superhero would change nothing.

Nothing at all.

CHAPTER TWO

DR S.A. MARSHALL was lounging again.

This time he sat on the edge of the large central desk, which was positioned in the wide corridor that separated the row of cubicles from the resus. area. He was leaning back with his weight resting easily on his hands, one of which was threatening to remove the receiver of one of the telephones he had displaced.

Kate felt as if she was being baited so she ignored him determinedly. She rubbed another square clean on the huge whiteboard beside the desk.

'Mrs Simmons, in cubicle three, is being admitted for obs and gynae observation with threatened premature labour. She's running a high temperature. Bloods and urine have been sent off but no results back yet.'

Kate looked around the circle of staff. She focused on Joe Millar.

'Mrs Joan Berry, cubicle two, is a seventy-three-year old who fell, while getting on a bus this morning, and has a probable fractured neck of femur. Joe, can you go with her to Radiology? Keep the cardiac monitor on. She has a history of angina and is pretty stressed at the moment.'

Kate scribbled the update of information on the whiteboard and continued through a list of minor cases which were at present keeping the cubicles occupied.

Sam let his thoughts wander. Now into the third week of his visit to St Matthew's, he felt quite at home in the emergency department. It had only taken a week or so for the strangeness to wear off. In fact, he felt more than at home. He was enjoying himself immensely.

The variety and severity of the cases available was proving as much as he'd hoped for. The list Kate was now updating for the change of shift was unusually ordinary, but he knew that would change before the day was much older. What was even better than the case load was the co-operation and encouragement he was receiving from the infirmary's consultant and other staff. Something about Sam or his intended career had fired a collective imagination. He knew he was the talking point for many departments and the enthusiastic acceptance had delighted him.

Of course, there were exceptions. Sam let his gaze focus on Kate Campbell with increased concentration. As if aware of the gaze, Kate turned away.

'Julian, could you have a look at cubicle five, please? Jason Duff is four years old. He decided to open a door, using a karate chop on the glass panel rather than the handle. No arterial involvement in the lacerations but he's not very co-operative so may need a general, rather than a local, anaesthetic for the suturing.'

'I would think that's rather more my decision than yours, wouldn't you, Kate?'

Sam winced inwardly at the casual put-down and noticed the exchange of glances between other staff members. His curiosity and sympathy were aroused but he also felt irritated by the way Kate accepted the barb. He watched the square set of her shoulders as she followed Julian Calder to cubicle five. Why didn't she stand up for herself? At least she could have delegated someone else to the task of assisting Julian. Sam eased himself off the desk, intent on following the pair.

There were a lot of things that puzzled him about Kate, and even his controlled persistence so far hadn't gained him much ground. But there was plenty of time and Sam had no intention of giving up. If nothing else, he was determined to discover why this woman stood out so convincingly amongst the huge numbers of people he had met in recent weeks.

The radio transmitter on the desk crackled into life as he moved away. Sam paused as a senior registrar, Louise Grant, took the call. He listened with interest as Louise took the details on a thirty-seven-year-old electrician who had suffered a flash burn when the fuse he'd been changing had exploded. The ETA was ten minutes. Louise caught his eye.

'Interested?'

'Sure. Burns are something I haven't had that much experience with.'

'Doesn't sound too bad, but I'll get someone from plastics down anyway and call you when he arrives.'

'Thanks. I'll be in cubicle five.'

Louise raised her eyebrows. The noise level from cubicle five had reached most areas of the department now. The overall consensus already was that a general anaesthetic would have been kinder on everyone involved. Sam was more than inclined to agree when he entered the cubicle, to find a struggling and swollen-faced child being held firmly by Kate and Margo as Julian finished infiltrating a large laceration with local anaesthetic. The child's mother stood by the top of the bed, looking firmly away from the scene.

Julian dropped the syringe into a kidney dish and stood up. 'I'll leave it up to you now, Kate. Suture those two larger ones—you can Steri-strip the rest.' He noticed Sam's presence and smiled with obvious relief. 'Coffee?' he suggested.

'I'm waiting for a burns case, coming in,' Sam replied. 'I'll catch you later.'

Kate moved a trolley closer to the bed with her foot. 'I'm going to put some stitches in your arm now, Jason,' she explained, 'but it's not going to hurt any more.'

'No. No. No!' the child shrieked. 'Don't touch!'

Kate eyed the child's mother. 'Could you hold his arm still for me?'

'I can't look,' the mother said through clenched teeth.

'You don't have to look,' Kate said patiently. 'Just hold Jason's wrist here, like this.' She glanced at the other nurse. 'Are you OK there, Margo?'

'I guess.' Margo sounded as though she also had clenched teeth. She was pinning Jason's other arm, as well as holding his head still. They might have managed except that the child's terror now negated the fact that he couldn't feel any pain. He brought his legs into his struggle and sent Kate's tray of suture material flying.

'Let him go,' Sam suggested quietly.

With renewed hope for escape Jason's screams subsided instantly and he sat up. Sam gently caught the child's uninjured arm as he scrambled from the bed.

'Hold on there, sport.' He swung the boy around

and collected him on his lap as he sat on the bed. 'I want to hear about this karate chop of yours. You're pretty tough, eh?'

Jason eyed the man who towered above him. He wasn't defeated yet and nodded confirmation vigorously.

'I want to go home. Now!'

'In a few minutes,' Sam agreed. 'I guess if you're so tough you're not scared of much.'

'Nah.'

'What about snakes?'

'Nah. I'd just hit them with a stick.'

'Spiders?' Sam nodded at Kate who had collected a new sterile pack. She moved some pillows to support Jason's wrist. Sam put his arm around the boy's shoulders casually, his hand steadying the arm as Kate began to apply Steri-strips to close a smaller wound. Jason tried to struggle but Sam's grip tightened just enough to let him know he couldn't win. The boy sniffed noisily and turned his face away from Kate.

'I'd squash spiders,' he told Sam fiercely. 'Splat! Just like that.'

'What about poisonous spiders? Where I come from we get lots of poisonous spiders.'

'I'd squash them too,' Jason stated. 'Or maybe I'd karate chop them—like I did to the door.'

Sam grinned at Jason's mother who rolled her eyes and sighed.

'What if you didn't see one on a dunny seat and sat on it?'

'What's a dunny?'

'A toilet,' Sam explained. 'An outside one. Usually in a little shed at the bottom of the garden.'

Jason nodded. 'My grandpa's got one like that. It smells.'

Kate's eyes widened at the turn of the conversation but she was too grateful for the respite the child's interest was giving her to make any comment. By the time Sam had finished singing a song about the Redback on the Dunny Seat she was tying off the last suture. With relief she reached for the gauze dressing Margo was holding, just as Louise poked her head around the curtain.

'Coming in now, Sam.'

'OK.' Sam stood, easing the child back onto the bed. 'Look after Kate while she puts your bandage on, sport,' he instructed their young patient. 'She's scared of spiders.'

It was a morning for small, wailing children. Kate dealt with a two-year-old child who had poked a piece of chewing-gum up his nose several days previously. Julian remained conspicuously absent and the ENT registrar who was called in was quick to recommend a general anaesthetic to remove the now-offensive blockage.

A six-year-old girl had fallen from a jungle gym at school and was quickly dispatched to radiology for confirmation of her collar-bone fracture. Kate had the beginnings of a headache by the time another two-year-old boy, Matthew, was rushed in by his frantic mother, having swallowed most of her bottle of paracetamol tablets. Kate was not going to allow this child's struggles to defeat her, and managed to administer a good dose of ipecac by dint of her determination and good timing as the toddler drew breath between screams. The boy became much quieter as he began to look green around the gills, and Kate knew the ordeal would soon be over.

Julian Calder appeared in the cubicle with Sam at this point. Julian picked up the chart with the recordings and observations Kate had noted on Matthew so far, but he didn't appear to be reading them.

'Second-degree burns to most of his face,' Sam was saying, 'but he was lucky enough to have his eyes and mouth closed. No airway burn.'

'Electrocution?' Julian was clearly more interested in Sam's case than the pale-faced boy, sitting on the bed. Kate hovered with a large basin.

'We couldn't find any entry or exit wounds. His arm was black but he had full sensation in his fingers.'

'What did plastics say?'

'It all looked superficial. Pain relief and dressings, re-evaluation in—' Sam stopped. He was watching Matthew with some interest. Julian shrugged and finally dropped his eyes to the chart he was holding.

Kate did try very hard to get into the right position with her basin. Neither she nor Matthew's mother could have foreseen the way the toddler threw himself forward nor predicted just how violent the episode of vomiting would be. With apparent startling accuracy the mixture of the large breakfast and at least a dozen paracetamol tablets landed squarely on the shiny perfection of Julian Calder's shoes.

There was a moment's stunned silence. Kate was grateful that she had to deal with Matthew, holding the boy's head over the basin as the effects of the ipecac continued. She had to press her lips together tightly at the roar of Sam's laughter that followed Julian's hissed expletive.

'Sorry, mate—but you should see your face!'

Kate didn't need to look. She knew that the expression of fury would be directed at her. She heard Sam's guffaws fade as he followed Julian's rapid exit from the cubicle. Kate stroked Matthew's head.

'We've got rid of all those nasty pills now,' she told him. 'You're doing really well.'

Kate took a break, having cleaned up cubicle two. The department was quiet and she ducked into the locker room to fetch her parka. It wasn't raining outside and she was desperate for a few minutes of fresh air. She caught sight of Julian, the white theatre gumboots at distinct odds with the pinstripe trousers, and hid a smile as she slipped out through the deserted ambulance bay doors.

The pedestrian crossing covered eight lanes of traffic but Kate hit the lights just right and it took only a minute to gain entry to her refuge—a tiny park, walled in by a high iron fence. It was only a small patch of green, tucked in behind the bus stops, half a dozen large trees and a couple of park benches, but Kate loved it. She sat on one of the benches, pulled her jacket around her uniform more securely, closed her eyes and took a deep breath of the crisp air. The bench suddenly rocked beneath her.

'G'day!'

'Oh, no!' Kate's eyes flew open. 'What are you doing here?'

Sam grinned. 'I followed you. I wanted to know what was preferable to coffee in the common room.'

'Fresh air,' Kate replied tartly. 'And a bit of solitude.'

'Bit cold.' Sam was wearing only a white coat over his shirt and jeans. Kate eyed his casual apparel with disapproval but said nothing. Just how long would it take for this man to realise she wasn't going to respond to his overtures of friendship? It was becoming increasingly difficult, thanks to his cheerful persistence. Kate had decided it wasn't really anything to do with any attraction he felt towards her. It was just the almost childlike aspect of the Australian's personality—an open interest in all the people he met and a lack of any social inhibition.

It was by now obvious to everyone what a social creature Dr S.A. Marshall was. He liked people and he enjoyed interacting with them. The genuine interest he felt gained a response that some found astonishing, especially some of the older consultants. Kate knew that even they regarded his social attributes with amused tolerance. She had overheard the head of surgery explain to a colleague that it was not entirely unexpected in someone descended from a colony of convicts. She knew the opinion would amuse Sam but she had no intention of adding to his enjoyment of his new environment. He was getting quite enough of that already.

The silence between them wasn't uncomfortable and Kate was just beginning to enjoy it when Sam unexpectedly broke it.

'Shame about those shoes.'

'Mmm.' Kate glanced sideways and caught Sam's serious gaze. The glance was held for a second before they both smiled. Kate felt a knot tighten within her. Nothing more needed to be said—the understanding was perfect. It was unnerving. Was this foreigner telepathic or something? Disturbed, Kate hurriedly stood.

'I've got to get back. I've only got ten minutes.'

'Aw, Kate.' Sam stood up reluctantly. 'How am I ever going to get to know you if you keep running away?'

Kate was silent. Sam fell into step beside her.

'I'm the new boy at school,' he said plaintively. 'I need to make some friends.'

'Why pick on me?' Kate responded. 'You've already made friends with half the hospital.' She threw Sam a curious glance as they made their way through the spiked iron gates. 'What on earth were you doing with Patsy in Reception yesterday?'

Sam laughed. He leaned against the traffic light pole as they waited for the signal to cross.

'She was teaching me to line-dance. Did you know she's in a troupe for over-fifties? They compete all over the place and wear matching fringed shirts and miniskirts and white cowboy hats and boots.' He laughed again. 'You should try it. It's a lot of fun.'

Kate shook her head, marching briskly past the waiting traffic. Patsy was a wiry, grim-faced woman who ruled the reception area with an iron fist. Even a busload of football hooligans couldn't faze her so the aggressive behaviour of minor cases, determined to jump the queue, didn't stand a chance. She had been in the department longer than anyone could remember, but even Kate had had no knowledge of her unusual passion. Sam had only been here for two weeks but Patsy's response to his interest was typical.

'Are they all like you in Australia?'

'Nope. I'm one of a kind.'

'Thank God for that.' Kate stepped sideways to skirt an incoming ambulance and bumped into her companion. He put out his hand to steady her but left it resting on her shoulder a little longer than necessary. He waited for the annoyed look he knew he would receive.

'I may have met an awful lot of people since I came here,' Sam told her, 'but it's you I'm really interested in, Katy.'

Kate shook her shoulder free. 'You're wasting your time, Sam,' she said quietly. 'There's nothing to interest you.'

'I would think that's rather more my decision than yours, wouldn't you, Kate?'

The echo of Julian's put-down brought a flush of colour to Kate's cheeks. 'Not in this case,' she said firmly. 'I thought I'd made things quite clear. I can't understand why you bother persisting.'

'I'm not quite sure of that myself just yet,' Sam replied easily. He watched Kate head into the department. 'But I'm damned sure I'm going to find out.'

Sam waved to Patsy as he went past her desk but his thoughts were still firmly on Kate Campbell. He knew she aroused a powerful protective instinct in him. Was that just a reflection of the protection she was clearly giving herself? Kate was a loner. Her only obvious friend in the department was Joe Millar and just as obviously their relationship was nothing more than friendship.

She was so determined not to attract attention— no make-up, the unfeminine hairstyle, the uniform which was a size too big and just that much longer than the other nurses wore theirs. Did she not realise it simply added to the waif-like effect of her fine features and those huge hazel eyes? Sam knew the emergency department director, Jeff Merrick, could see past the coolly professional barrier behind which Kate enclosed herself and had a great respect and fondness for his senior nurse.

And Julian Calder. Had he been genuinely interested or had he possibly just tried to bulldoze his way through a rejection that was an affront to a well-displayed male ego? Sam was intrigued. A keen observer of life, Sam was an expert in using even a spare few seconds to add to his knowledge of those around him. He could see and hear nuances in relationships, even when deliberately concentrating on something else.

Sam had never bothered trying to analyse this ability. If he had he might have attributed it to his upbringing. His father had died when Sam was too young to remember him and he had been raised by his mother, grandmother and three older sisters. The feminine outlook on life he had acquired had been rapidly suppressed once he'd started school, but the influence had remained and Sam was far more sensitive than his outward appearances advertised.

He browsed through the list on the whiteboard. If the department was busy he helped wherever needed, but otherwise he was in the unique position of being able to pick the cases he was most interested in. Right now his interest was still focused on a staff member rather than any patients. If it had been just female companionship or even a sexual relationship that Sam had been after he was quite well aware the pickings were rich and probably easy, but Sam had dabbled enough to know he was no longer interested in anything ordinary.

There was something rather unusual about Kate—something very well hidden. Even her voice was intriguing. She was always quietly spoken but with an unmistakable authority and an unusual lilt to some of her words, as though an accent hadn't quite been lost. Whatever the mystery was, it was affecting Sam like a rather powerful magnet. Perhaps he just needed a more unusual strategy in order to try and persuade Kate that friendship was at least worth considering.

Kate knew she was being followed almost as soon as she got off the bus. A quick glance behind her as she maintained her steady pace only served to push her mental alarm button more firmly. The shadowy figure was large, obviously male and was shrouded against the heavy rain by an oilskin parka, the hood pulled well over his face. He was carrying nothing, not even a shopping bag or a briefcase, which might suggest it was simply coincidence he was going in the same direction.

Kate automatically and unnecessarily crossed the road, noting with dismay that both pedestrian and vehicular traffic was sparse. Most of the suburb's residents had been home for some time, the curtains drawn eagerly to shut out another cold, wet night. Kate wished she hadn't taken the time to stay in the department and help Joe organise the rosters for the next month.

Another glance revealed that her potential assailant had also crossed the road and Kate knew she had to make a decision. She was only a few hundred yards

from her home. Should she make a run for it? The
footsteps behind her were closer now, the nearest
house dark and possibly unoccupied. Kate felt the
edge of panic suddenly recede. She was trained to
cope with exactly this situation. It was time to put
her training into practice.

Kate stepped smoothly to one side and changed
direction, crossing the street again. Her pursuer
dodged the car that went past and was running by
the time he made the opposite kerb. Kate turned,
dropping her shoulder-bag at the same moment her
assailant raised his arm. Instinctively, she grabbed his
wrist with her left hand, throwing her right arm in a
winding power curve over the imprisoned wrist. Her
body wound itself inside his outstretched arm as her
right leg moved to hook his. Kate experienced a flash
of satisfaction at the clean throw she achieved as her
heavy assailant hit the ground with a resounding
thud, but she had no intention of savouring the moment. Now was the time to run.

Her flight was stilled, however, by the loud groan
that came from the prone figure. There was something in the voice familiar enough to make her pause
and peer under the hood of the oilskin.

'I don't believe it!'

The figure groaned again, his eyes tightly shut.

'You were following me again,' Kate shouted fu-
riously. 'You bloody idiot. I could have hurt you!'

'You have. Oh-h-h.' Sam opened one eye and
peered at Kate warily.

'Get up,' Kate ordered. 'It's pouring with rain.'

'I can't,' Sam groaned. 'I think I have severe spi-
nal injuries.'

'Rot.' But Kate's tone belied her sudden anxiety.

What if she really had injured him? She had been thrown herself, countless times, but her landings had been protected by crash mats. The pavement was a very different surface and Sam was a lot heavier than she was. Kate bit her lip.

'Are you really hurt?' she asked cautiously.

Sam groaned again.

'Where?'

'All over. Feel me.'

'No, thanks. Not unless you can be a bit more specific. Do you need an ambulance?'

'Quite probably. Jeez, Kate! Where did you learn to do that?'

'Never mind.' Kate was watching the car pull to a halt beside them. She would have to hope that Sam would be taken to a hospital other than St Matthew's. Even she might not be able to live with the embarrassment this incident could cause. The driver leapt from his car, clutching a cellphone.

'Do you need the police, love? Or an ambulance?'

'That won't be necessary.' To Kate's astonishment, Sam managed to rise quite smoothly to his feet. 'Thanks, anyway, mate. I'll watch where I walk in future.'

Kate's relief had turned to anger by the time the man was back in his car.

'You're lucky I don't flatten you again,' she informed Sam irately. 'What the hell do you think you're playing at?'

Sam was rubbing his arm. 'Perhaps you've just dislocated my shoulder after all.'

Kate bent to pick up her bag. 'Well, if it's any comfort to you I'll probably be rather stiff tomorrow myself.' She stretched her back, before beginning to move. A soak in a hot bath might be enough of a cure.

'Do you live around here?' Sam began to follow her.

'That's none of your business.' Kate walked on. She couldn't believe he had the nerve to continue following her.

'Aren't you going to take me home?' Sam queried. 'For a bandage and some brandy?'

Kate eyed Sam carefully. He was still rubbing his shoulder and he was limping slightly. Probably a put-on, Kate thought. But what if it wasn't?

'I'd settle for a cup of tea.'

'I'm sure you would. Why don't you go home and have one?'

'I'm lost,' Sam replied cheerfully. 'You're my only hope of shelter before I catch pneumonia.' She could tell he was grinning at her, even without looking. 'It comes on a lot faster after a shock, you know. I'm kind of wet as well.'

Kate said nothing. She had never allowed anybody into the home she now had. Why on earth was she considering it now? She bit her lip again.

'At least let me call a taxi,' Sam suggested. 'Or you can call a taxi and I'll wait out on the doorstep. In the rain. And the dark. And the cold. And—'

'Oh, all right,' Kate snapped. 'Stop grovelling.'

'I never grovel.' Sam sounded offended. 'I am just charmingly persuasive. Hey, do you really live around here?'

Even in the dark and rain the well-kept, tall Victorian terraced houses were impressive. The well-polished doorknockers gleamed under the streetlights, the iron railing fences neatly sectioning one from the next. Kate paused beside the nearest one.

'It's not quite as impressive as it looks,' she warned him. Instead of heading to the front door, Kate turned off the path and headed down a flight of steps that ran parallel to the railing fence and finished well below street level. She unlocked a door between two small windows, glancing sharply at Sam when he chuckled.

'It fits,' he explained. 'You live in a burrow!'

Kate pushed the door open, without responding. She hoped she wasn't making the biggest mistake of her life but it was too late to turn back now.

'Leave your coat by the door,' she ordered. 'I haven't got any brandy but I think I can manage a cup of tea.' Kate was moving quickly as she spoke, turning on lamps and drawing the curtains. A large, fat black cat twined itself around her ankles, complaining.

'I know, I know.' Kate bent to scratch him behind the ears and then scooped him into her arms. 'I'll get your dinner, Bartholemew. I got held up.'

Sam's eyes were roving eagerly. The bedsitting room was tiny, but contained a wealth of information about its occupant. There was colour everywhere. A bright patchwork quilt covered the bed, bunches of silk flowers topped unusual ceramic pots and a mobile of iridescent butterflies hovered in the corner. The colour was added to and given richness by the huge bookshelf that completely lined one wall and was stuffed to overflowing with books. Sam happily skimmed the titles of one shelf.

'Is there anything you don't read?' he called.

Kate poked her head through the door that led to

the tiny galley kitchen. She was holding an opened can of cat food. 'Not much,' she said casually. 'How do you take your tea?'

'Milk and sugar, ta.' Sam was moving towards the small stereo unit and the stack of CDs. Kate found the frank examination of her home more disturbing than she had anticipated. She hurried back to pour the tea. When she returned, carrying two mugs, she found Sam chuckling again.

'What's so funny?' she demanded. 'You do realise you're invading my privacy here?'

'Sorry.' Sam was still smiling. 'I was expecting some folk and classical music and look...' He riffled through the handful of CDs he held. 'Meatloaf, Queen—even the Rolling Stones. You're into some heavy rock.'

'It's not as weird as line-dancing,' Kate retorted defensively. 'Here's your tea. I'll ring for a taxi.'

Bartholemew had finished his dinner by the time Kate picked up her own drink. Sam was sitting on her bed, she noticed with dismay. She should feel angry but instead she felt that knot in her stomach again and was aware of a distinct increase in her heart rate. She frowned as the cat ignored her in favour of joining Sam on the bed.

Kate remained standing. 'Your taxi shouldn't be too long.'

'I love your room,' Sam told her. Bartholemew's head was completely hidden by the large hand as Sam gently rubbed the cat's ears. 'Do you live here alone?'

'That's—'

'None of my business. I know.' Sam laughed easily. 'Why don't you just give in, Katy? Tell me about yourself.'

'Why don't you just give up, Sam? Can't you take a hint?'

'Nope. I'm an incurable sticky-beak.'

'A what?'

'Sticky-beak. Nosy Parker. I'm interested in people, Kate. I like to know what makes them tick. I'd like to know what makes you tick.'

Kate sighed. 'How's your shoulder?'

Sam grinned. 'That's another thing. Are you a champion in kung fu or something?'

'Judo, actually. I have been a member of the British women's team. I coach juniors these days.' Kate flushed slightly under the admiring stare she was receiving. 'I wouldn't have been able to throw you if you'd been expecting it. It was the element of surprise that made it work.'

'I was surprised, all right,' Sam agreed. 'Do you do that to unsuspecting men very often?'

'That was the first time,' Kate admitted. 'I don't get followed very often. Why did you raise your arm like that, anyway? I thought you were about to hit me.'

'I was about to wave,' Sam said ruefully. 'I didn't think you'd seen me.'

The sound of a hooter from the street above surprised Kate. The taxi had been quick. What surprised her more, however, was the pang of disappointment she felt.

'I'd better go,' Sam said cheerfully. 'Thanks for the tea, Kate. And I'm sorry I gave you a fright.'

'I'm the one who ought to apologise,' Kate murmured. 'I guess I overreacted.' She handed him his still dripping parka, then reached for the doorhandle. 'By the way, thanks for your help with Jason this morning.'

'A pleasure.' Sam winced slightly as he eased his arm into his jacket sleeve. 'Your stitching was something to see. A plastic surgeon wouldn't have done a neater job.'

Kate smiled. 'I doubt that.' She stood back as Sam passed her then raised her voice a little. 'One other thing.'

Sam paused on the second step. 'What's that?'

'I'm not scared of spiders.'

Sam stepped back down again. He turned so that he was facing Kate, his face only inches from hers. For a horrified instant she thought he was going to kiss her. She watched his lips move as he spoke very quietly.

'I know that,' he said carefully. 'You're scared of something, Katy Campbell. But it isn't spiders.'

CHAPTER THREE

'CLASSIC "bucket handle" displacement. Look at that disruption to the sacroiliac joint.' A finger tapped the X-ray image on the viewing screen with rapid jabs.

'No wonder he's losing volume so fast. The veins around the sacroiliac joints are the most likely candidates for major haemorrhage.'

'Another good reason to go for external fixation. Any mucking about with a retroperitoneal haematoma would release any tamponade effect. Good way to start a catastrophic and uncontrollable haemorrhage.'

Kate glanced over at the group of doctors, crowding the screen, as she hooked the new bag of IV fluid onto the pole in readiness. The first one was almost depleted. Her eyes returned to the monitor screens above her patient at the hiss of the blood-pressure cuff, inflating automatically.

'BP now ninety-five over sixty,' she told Margo calmly. The junior nurse recorded the measurement then looked up to the ECG screen to note the heart rate and rhythm. Kate was aware that a new image had been clipped to the viewing screen in front of the consultants.

'That's a better view,' she heard someone say. 'We've got fractures of the superior and inferior pubic rami.'

'Anything on rectal examination?'

'Negative.'

Kate caught the anxious gaze of their patient above his oxygen mask. The voice was too muffled to understand so Kate lifted the mask a little.

'I've got to go, Nurse.'

'Not yet, Mr Lye. We've got to sort you out first.'

'It's urgent!'

Kate smiled reassuringly. Judging by the well-cut suit, the lap-top computer and the briefcase which the patient had come in with, Jeremy Lye was a businessman. Perhaps it had been an urgent appointment that had made him play chicken with the morning's rush-hour traffic. The thirty-two-year-old had lost in a big way when he had been clipped by the delivery van.

'You don't understand,' Jeremy Lye said with embarrassment. 'I need to pee.'

'OK. Sorry.' Kate checked her patient's pelvic area again briefly. Pelvic fractures commonly caused internal injuries. Trying to urinate with urethral damage could lead to further complications, but there was still no sign of external bleeding and she knew the rectal examination hadn't given any cause for concern. She tucked a plastic bottle discreetly under the sheet.

The doctors were still in earnest conversation when Kate moved over to them a minute later.

'Julian? Mr Lye is complaining of an urgent need to urinate—'

'Get him a bottle, then,' Julian interrupted. 'You're the nurse, aren't you?'

Kate's breath out was almost a sigh. She saw Sam's quick glance in her direction. 'I have,' she informed Julian. 'He's not able to pass anything.'

'Well, why didn't you say so in the first place?' Julian threw a long-suffering look at Sam, who turned immediately to Kate.

'There's no evidence of urethral bleeding, is there?'

'No.' Kate shook her head. 'I've got a catheter trolley ready.'

Sam glanced back at Julian. 'Shall I do the honours?'

'All yours, old chap.'

The orthopaedic surgeon finally turned away from the X-rays. He followed Julian back to the patient's bedside.

'What's the BP doing?' he queried.

'Could be better.' Julian increased the flow rate on both IV lines.

'We'd better get our external fixation sorted. Ever done one, Sam?'

'Never.' Sam was still concentrating on his task. 'I don't think we've got any urethral damage here. Access to the bladder is easy enough.' When he looked over to the surgeon his gaze had a distinct glint. 'Are you going to do the fixation here?'

'I rather thought you might like to,' the surgeon told him. 'Could be a useful technique out in the wilds.'

Sam's grin was enthusiastic. 'I'll get scrubbed again.'

Kate was still handling the other end of the urethral catheter. She watched the slow trickle of faintly bloodstained fluid. 'Minimal urine output,' she reported.

'Give Urology a call,' Julian ordered her. 'We'll

need surgery pretty sharpish if it's a ruptured bladder.'

'BP's still falling. Eighty over fifty-five. Pulse rate up to one-twenty,' Margo advised.

'Is that oxygen a hundred per cent?'

'Yes.'

Kate caught the increasingly agitated patient's hand before he could pull out his IV line. Julian was holding his shoulders to prevent him trying to sit up. 'Steady on, there, old chap.' He turned away briefly. 'Where's Roger?'

'He's assessing the asthma case in bed one,' Kate informed him. 'They may need to ventilate her.'

'Well, we need him here. Go and get him, Kate. Tell him we need to sedate and ventilate Mr Lye here before we can stabilise him.'

Kate felt as if she hadn't stopped running ever since she'd arrived for her shift that morning. The heavy stream of minor cases had been punctuated by several serious injuries, such as that suffered by Jeremy Lye. With their patient successfully intubated, Kate watched with interest as Sam screwed the four pins into the iliac crests on either side of the patient's pelvis. He then began to assemble the frame of rods and bolts to connect them under the direction of the orthopaedic surgeon.

'If this fails to control the haemorrhage we'll have to go for some angiography,' the surgeon told Sam, 'but we'll do a CT scan first and adjust the tension on this contraption.'

'This would have to be a lot more effective in controlling haemorrhage than a MAST suit.' Sam referred to the pressure garment initially applied to Jeremy Lye's lower body and legs at the accident scene. 'Trouble is, you can get major pelvic injuries with almost no external signs, and we don't fly around with X-ray gear.'

The surgeon nodded. 'By the time you get swelling and bruising around the area you're already looking at some rather profound blood loss. Still, you must get pretty good at general assessment under those conditions. Not like us—we get to click our fingers and have specialist consults and investigations from any area. I rather envy the responsibility and variety you're going to get.' He checked the final bolt Sam had tightened. 'That's good. I could swear you've done this before.'

Sam grinned as he shook his head. He stripped off his gloves as he stood back to admire his handiwork. 'Nope. Almost needed one myself, though.'

'Really?'

'Yeah. Last night.' Sam rubbed his lower back reflectively. 'Took a bit of a tumble.'

Kate knew she was blushing even before Sam winked at her. Any hope that he might have spared her embarrassment, by not mentioning the incident, evaporated. The department had just been too busy so far today for anything but purely professional communication. At least Julian and Margo were now busy with an overdose case in bed two. Joe had accompanied the young asthmatic up to the intensive care unit. The anaesthetist, Roger, had noticed the wink and her unusual colour, however.

'You all right, Kate?'

'I'm fine, thanks.'

'Good.' He eyed her for a second, as though puzzled, then he turned back to the monitors. 'This chap's doing better, too. BP's stable.'

The curtains opened to admit the urology consultant and his registrar, and Kate used the distraction to begin tidying up the considerable debris they had already collected. Turning to deposit soiled drapes into the linen hamper, she found that Sam was grinning at her. She glared back.

'I suppose you intend to let the whole department know about last night,' she whispered angrily.

'My lips are sealed,' Sam whispered back in reply. Then he spoke more firmly. 'On one condition.'

'Which is?'

'You come out with me for a meal tonight.'

'No.' Kate shoved the linen into the bag.

'A drink, then?'

Kate was silent. Sam massaged his shoulder rather obviously. 'I think it's time for a cup of tea. In the common room maybe. A cup of tea and a bit of sympathy.'

'This is blackmail,' Kate hissed.

'Too right.' Sam glanced towards the other consultants then flashed another quick grin at Kate. 'Six o'clock?'

Kate sighed in exasperation. 'I suppose I'll have to.'

'That's the spirit.' Sam dropped his gloves into the rubbish bin. 'I'll be looking forward to it as well.'

The trackpants had to go. Kate eyed them with sudden distaste as she changed after work. The pants and her pullover were her out-of-hours uniform at this time of year. What could she wear instead? It had been so long since Kate had considered clothing in anything but terms of comfort and warmth that she felt at a complete loss.

She knew what had triggered the dissatisfaction, however, and felt irritated. Sam was so pushy! And persistent. It was disturbing. It wasn't just that her routine was being disrupted—it was the wider ramifications. Like being made aware that her clothing was really not what she enjoyed wearing at all. If she hadn't agreed to go for a drink with Sam that awareness could have stayed well buried.

Kate pulled on her oilskin with a sigh. What did it matter? There were plenty of pubs where no one was going to notice her standard of dress and, having forced her into accepting his invitation, Sam would probably lose interest anyway. Maybe he had already.

It was only five-fifty when Kate made for the main entrance but Sam was already there, waiting. He held a flower. A single white daisy with a rather bent stem.

'It's for you,' he told her gravely.

Kate tried to look impressed. 'You shouldn't have!'

'I didn't, really. It must have fallen out of someone's bouquet outside. It reminded me of you.'

'Why?'

'Well, there it was. All alone. Waiting to be picked up.'

'By you?'

'Exactly.'

'Tell me, does your ego match your shoe size?'

Sam looked down the considerable length of his body. His tone was dubious. 'My feet are kind of big.'

'Exactly.'

They stared at each other and again Kate felt that

moment of connection before they both smiled. With unspoken agreement they headed outside. Last night's rain had been replaced by a heavy fog. It was damp and dismal but Kate didn't mind in the least.

'So. Where are you taking me?'

Sam looked surprised. 'I thought you were taking me. I have no idea what's around here.'

'I thought Julian took you somewhere.'

'He did—but it was full of hospital folk.'

Kate caught his glance. His consideration of her possible lack of enthusiasm to be seen by her colleagues surprised her, given his threat to broadcast her treatment of him last night. Yet it wasn't surprising at all. Dr S.A. Marshall was a puzzle. He was egotistical, over-confident and exasperatingly pushy, but it seemed somehow to only add to his charm. The only explanation Kate could find was this uncanny ability he had to tune in to his emotional environment. Was he like this with everyone he met or could it be something special that might apply only to herself? Kate shied away from the dangerous thought.

'We're bound to find somewhere if we keep walking. One thing London's not short of is pubs.'

'As long as it isn't anything swanky,' Sam warned. 'I don't reckon we'd be allowed in for champagne cocktails at the Savoy.'

'No.' Again Kate felt a surge of dislike for her appearance. She looked as grey and dismal as the weather.

'I guess I ought to get a pair of pinstripes,' Sam suggested. 'I could probably scrub up quite well if I gave it a go.'

Kate eyed the blue jeans that effortlessly kept pace

with her own brisk stride. She shook her head. 'You wouldn't suit pinstripes,' she murmured. 'Too ordinary.'

Sam didn't appear to have heard. 'What about that place? I can't read the sign in this fog. Something about a goose.'

They entered a typical and well-patronised London pub. A darts game was going on in one corner. The flames of an open fire gave the decoration of horse-brasses a rosy tinge, the noise level was high and it took several minutes to gain the attention of a barmaid.

'What'll it be?'

Sam raised an eyebrow at Kate.

'I'll have a lager, thanks.'

'Ah! I knew we had at least one thing in common.' Sam turned back to the barmaid. 'Two lagers, ta, and a bag of chips. What flavours have you got?'

The barmaid looked nonplussed. 'We don't do chips.'

Kate saw the direction of Sam's gaze. 'He means crisps,' she explained to the barmaid. 'We'll have Marmite flavour. He's Australian.'

The barmaid's smile broadened. 'That explains a lot.'

'What could she mean?' Sam's tone was innocent as he watched her reach for the chilled bottles of lager and flip off the caps. 'Do they really have Marmite-flavoured chips?'

'Crisps,' Kate corrected. 'Chips are the hot things you get at the fish and chip shops. And, yes, they do come in Marmite.'

Sam grinned. 'Can you get jam-flavoured ones as well?'

Kate returned the smile. 'Give them time.'

There were no tables available but Kate commandeered a single bar stool. Sam stood beside her, his elbow resting on the bar-top. 'Cheers! Hey, these chips are great.'

'Crisps.'

Sam ignored the correction. 'They remind me of my school lunches. Mum used to make Marmite sandwiches and put squashed chips in them as well.'

'That's gross!' Kate took a sip of her lager. 'Are you homesick, then?'

Sam considered. 'I miss the space,' he told her. 'I don't like the crowds in Sydney even, and that's a small town compared to London. I can't wait to head for the outback again.' He eyed Kate. 'You'd love it.'

'Oh?'

'Someone like you would be perfect. Strong character, exceptional medical skills. You'd have a lot more scope to use them and you wouldn't have to put up with the nonsense you get from the likes of Julian Calder.'

Kate dropped her eyes. It was the first time she had heard her personality described as a strong character. It gave her reserve a dignity she rather liked.

'What's keeping you here, Katy?'

'I love my job,' Kate said defensively.

'There's more to life than work,' Sam stated. 'And you haven't got any close friends.'

'I have so!'

'Who?'

'Joe.'

'Hmm.' Sam gave her a very speculative look. 'Nice, safe friendship, that.'

Kate looked away. 'I don't know what you mean.'

Sam waved the empty crisp bag at the barmaid and signalled for another. 'My older sister, Lizzy, had a friend at university,' he said casually. 'Mike. Really nice guy. He was gay.'

'So?'

'So Lizzy told me once that he was the perfect friend as far as she was concerned. No competition for the same men, no possible sexual agenda to worry about and an interest in and sympathy with a woman's point of view.'

Kate was silent. Joe's private life was exactly that. Private. She knew for a fact from conversations in the locker room that the other staff had no idea of Joe's relationship preferences. It was typical that Sam was so aware of what they had missed, but Kate was not prepared to discuss it. She respected Joe's privacy. The bond of their personal reserve had been what had generated their friendship in the first place.

'So, who else?'

'Sorry?' Kate's thoughts returned instantly to her companion.

'Who are your other close friends?'

'That's none of your business.'

Sam grinned. 'OK. Well, there's more to life than work and close friends.'

'Such as?'

'Adventure!' Sam wiggled his eyebrows enthusiastically and his matching grin made Kate splutter into her lager.

'Have you always been a fan of Crocodile Dundee?' she managed to ask.

Sam leaned close. His voice was a conspiratorial

whisper. 'Don't tell anyone,' he murmured, 'but Crocodile Dundee has always been a fan of mine.'

Kate laughed. With the laughter came a sense of unusual relief. Unusual enough to make her break one of her cast-iron rules and reveal personal information. 'I get plenty of adventure,' she declared.

'Oh, yeah? What? Wearing white pyjamas and throwing people around in kung fu?'

'It's judo,' Kate said impatiently. 'And I wasn't talking about that. I go backpacking in my holidays. Places where I know I'm not going to find tourists. I've been to Israel, Egypt and Turkey, and right now I'm saving up to go to Africa next year.'

Sam was staring at her. 'Close your mouth,' she ordered him.

'I'm impressed,' Sam said seriously. 'You don't go by yourself, do you?'

'Of course.' Kate drained the last of her lager. 'I've got no close friends, remember? I use public transport and backpackers' accommodation. There's always company if I want it. Besides, I can take care of myself.'

Unconsciously, Sam rubbed at his shoulder. 'I guess you can. OK, then...' He narrowed his eyes as though about to pull out his ace. 'There's more to life than work, close friends and adventure.'

Kate grinned. 'Such as?' She was enjoying the verbal sparring. In fact, she couldn't remember when she had last had such a stimulating conversation.

Sam pursed his lips thoughtfully. 'Love,' he pronounced calmly.

Kate grinned again. 'I love my job. There you go, we're back to square one. I win.'

'Not fair,' Sam protested. 'Let's make it best out

of three.' He pointed to her empty glass. 'Can I get you another?'

'No, I've got to go.' Kate slid off her stool. 'I've got a kung fu class this evening.'

It felt odd, wearing her holiday jeans in to work the next morning. They seemed to fit more snugly than she remembered, and she was grateful for the over-sized dark sweater that covered the way they clung to her slim hips. Things felt more normal once she was back in her uniform but the department felt odd. It took a while but eventually Kate realised it was because Sam was absent. Had she really become so aware of his presence in the last few weeks? She hadn't thought so, particularly when the department was as busy as it was now. Any doubt she had was dispelled a short time later with the lift in her spirits when she spotted Sam in conversation with Jeff Merrick.

Kate paused to scribble some blood-test results onto the whiteboard, moving aside as she wrote to allow Joe access to one of the desk telephones. She smiled in response to Joe's greeting but her gaze returned to the two consultants. Sam grinned and winked at her and Kate felt an absurd wave of pleasure. Joe was now talking on the phone, requesting a paediatric registrar to look at a toddler with severe gastroenteritis, but Kate was aware of his scrutiny. The fact that Sam's greeting had given her more pleasure than Joe's made Kate feel somehow disloyal so she smiled at Joe again as she moved away. Collecting a hospital gown from a shelf, Kate handed it to Jude.

'Cubicle five,' she instructed the young nurse.

'We've got a fourteen-year-old girl, Sophie Nairn, with abdominal pain. Get her changed and take her temperature and BP. Julian's going to have a look at her in a minute. Stay with her. She got brought in from school and has a friend with her, but her mother hasn't been contacted yet.'

Sam's laughter made Kate look in his direction yet again. The usually quiet department director was also laughing. It really was astonishing, the effect this newcomer had on people. It was quite impossible not to respond and Kate knew how hard she had tried. She saw Joe helping an elderly man towards a cubicle. She had never thought of their friendship in the terms of safety, as Sam had suggested. It struck her now how correct he might be. Her relationship with the male nurse was well established and comforting, but a conversation with Joe could never have the effect that last night's session with Sam had had.

Kate had been bursting with energy by the time she'd arrived at the judo club. The junior team seemed to have enjoyed the vigorous instruction as much as she had, judging by the unusual amount of laughter which had been generated. She could still feel the bubbles of energy within her. Perhaps Dr Marshall's enthusiasm for life was contagious. And perhaps she wouldn't be so ungracious in accepting another invitation to spend time with him. If there *was* another invitation, of course, which was unlikely.

The brief but totally uncharacteristic train of thought returned instantly to professional matters when a paramedic team came crashing unexpectedly through the ambulance bay doors.

'Sorry—problems with the transmitter—we couldn't radio in.'

Kate reached the trolley first. She put her hands on the knees of the convulsing child to stop them hitting the metal side-bars. 'What happened?' she queried as they moved.

'Mother found her convulsing. Five-year-old girl, Taylor Harns, with a shunted hydrocephalus. Fell from a tree three days ago and was admitted then.'

Jeff Merrick and Sam joined the team in the resus. area.

'How long has this being going on?' Sam asked.

The paramedic checked his watch. 'It's twenty-five minutes since we got the call.'

Jeff spoke to the mother as Sam suctioned the girl's airway. Louise Grant and Joe arrived as the paramedic team left.

'She lost consciousness after the fall for about a minute,' the mother explained. 'They said she had some bruising but no skull fractures. She was kept in hospital overnight but allowed home the next day. She seemed fine.'

Jeff Merrick signalled Kate. 'Get her notes pulled and contact the paediatric neurologist involved.' He turned to Sam. 'Have you got an IV line going?'

'Almost.' Sam was completing the difficult task thanks to Joe steadying the twitching arm.

'Any focal neurological signs, Louise?'

'No.'

Kate was back quickly. 'The notes were still in the ward, waiting for a discharge summary. The registrar's bringing them down now.'

'What's her weight?' Jeff asked Mrs Harns.

The woman shook her head. 'I'm not sure.'

'I'd guess around twenty kilos,' Sam suggested. 'Fifty pounds or so.'

Jeff nodded agreement. 'Let's give her 6 mg diazepam, IV, over five minutes.'

Kate moved to draw up the drug. The seizure stopped within two minutes of its administration, at which time the paediatric neurology registrar arrived. The consensus of consultant opinion was that Taylor should be transferred to the ICU, and Jeff Merrick went to make the phone call himself. Kate paused to comfort Taylor's mother.

'She's supposed to wear her crash hat outside all the time. And she's certainly not allowed to climb trees. She's been doing so well lately.'

'All children test their limits,' Kate told her, 'especially when the limits need to be more confining, as in Taylor's case. You can't watch them all the time. Don't blame yourself.'

Julian and another registrar entered the resus. area. 'We've got a head injury coming in. Two minutes. Fall from scaffolding, second-storey level, and hit his head on a bar on the way down.'

'How's Sophie?' Kate had been concerned about the pale and very frightened schoolgirl she had seen earlier.

'I don't think there's too much wrong.' Julian was offhand. 'Could be appendicitis but she's not very co-operative with any sort of history. I'll have another look at her when the bloods come back.'

The staff numbers were good when the head-injury case came in. Kate pulled the curtains to screen the activity from the Harns' end.

'We'll get Taylor shifted in a minute,' she told the

child's mother. 'I'll come up with you to the intensive care unit.'

'What will they do to her there?'

'I imagine they'll want to do a CT scan of her head before anything else. It's the best place for close monitoring and evaluation, anyway.' Kate's gaze was on the drowsy child. She saw the signs of the seizure returning even before Louise, who was keeping an eye on the child's airway. Sam was still standing aside from the resuscitation of the young builder with the head injury and Kate called him over calmly.

'We'll repeat the diazepam,' Sam instructed. 'And add phenytoin—400 mg at a rate of 25–50 mg per minute. Keep a close eye on her blood pressure and ECG.'

It was another twenty minutes before Taylor was transferred to ICU, by which time the seriously injured builder had already been taken for an urgent CT scan. Jeff Merrick returned to check Taylor just before she left and nodded at Sam's description of the additional treatment.

'Diazepam is short-acting. A second dose is almost routine. Phenytoin's a good choice for a longer-term anticonvulsant. You don't want sedation when you need to monitor the level of consciousness post-head trauma.'

Kate resisted the urge for a few minutes of fresh air when she returned from ICU. Instead, she went to see Sophie.

'Is your mum not here yet?'

'No.'

Kate was surprised. The girl had been in the department for over an hour now. Something about the glance Sophie shared with her friend alerted Kate's instincts. She wrapped a BP cuff around the girl's slim arm.

'How's the tummy?'

'Not so bad. Can I go now?'

'Not yet.' Kate noted the sheen of perspiration on Sophie's forehead and reached for her wrist.

'I'm all right—honestly.'

'Something made you faint at school. We need to check it out.' Kate made a note of the vital signs.

'It's nothing. Just my period or something.'

'Oh? Are you bleeding?'

'No. I don't know.' Again the look passed between the teenagers.

'We'd better have a look.' Kate turned to Sophie's friend. 'Why don't you go and see the ladies in Reception? They'll show you where you can get a cup of tea or a Coke.'

Alone with the girl, Kate made a quick examination. 'Sophie, is there any chance you might be pregnant?'

'No!' The girl gasped in pain suddenly and screwed her eyes shut.

'It's important we know,' Kate told her quietly. 'We'll find out, anyway, but it could have an effect on how quickly we can treat you.'

Tears escaped the tightly shut eyelids but the girl simply shook her head. Kate gave her hand a reassuring squeeze. 'I'll be back in a minute, Sophie.'

It didn't take long to find Sam. 'Could you have a look at Sophie Nairn in cubicle five for me, please?'

Sam's gaze flicked to the whiteboard. 'That's Julian's possible appendicitis, isn't it?'

'Her BP's falling and she's in a lot of pain,' Kate said.

Sam frowned. 'We should page Julian, I suppose. I'm not sure where he is.'

'She's been here for over an hour,' Kate responded. 'I think it could be a ruptured ectopic pregnancy.'

Sam didn't hesitate. Kate followed him a minute later, having located Sophie's blood-test results. Sam was sitting on the side of the bed, holding Sophie's hand. The girl was crying.

'My mum will kill me if she finds out.'

Sam nodded at Kate. 'Give the obs and gynae folks a call, Kate. Jeff Merrick was right about your instincts.'

It was ridiculous to feel so disappointed. Kate had been fighting off Sam's persistent attempts to gain her attention, but now that she had given in, just a little, the persistence had ebbed. He wasn't any less friendly. He just seemed more casual, their conversations less personal.

When Kate escaped to the little park behind the bus stops for a break two days later she found the atmosphere of refuge had been spoiled. Suddenly she didn't want to be sitting there alone and she felt angry that the pleasure had gone.

She'd been right all along. It had only needed a little time with her for Sam to realise there was nothing to interest him. That was to be expected. In fact, that was what she had wanted. So why did she now feel let down? More than let down. Rejected.

Kate gave herself a mental shake. What did she want? A friendship with someone so capable of disrupting her defences? A friendship that had the dangerous potential to become something else? Kate denied it vigorously, but a niggling thought wouldn't be entirely suppressed. What if, after all this time, something might have changed? The something she hadn't thought she would even want to explore ever again?

She felt thoroughly disgruntled by the time her shift was over. Spending the last hour with an overdose case, who was convinced that the emergency department staff were trying to kill him, didn't help. Security had to be called to help subdue the abusive patient but even then it had proved impossible to get any charcoal into him. He denied any heroin abuse and they had no idea what the tablets purchased on the street had been. The infusion of Narcan had been very slow to produce any effects.

Kate couldn't wait to get home. Tomorrow was Sunday, her first day off in more than a week, and she intended to spend it curled up with a good book. Several good books, maybe.

The knock on her door at ten on Sunday morning was startling. Kate was even more startled to find Sam, standing at the bottom of her steps.

'G'day!'

'Hi!' Kate automatically suppressed her smile but she could feel the corners of her mouth twitch.

'It's your day off,' Sam informed her.

'I know that.'

'I thought I'd have one, too.'

'Fair enough.'

'I thought it was a good day for sightseeing.'

'There's a lot to see,' Kate agreed. 'Where are you going?'

Sam's grin was nothing short of cheeky. 'Where are you going to take me?'

'What makes you assume I'm going to take you anywhere?' Kate fought off a sudden surge of relief.

'It was the best of three, remember? I can't let you get away without a rematch.'

'I suppose I'll have to, then.' Kate grinned. 'I'll just get my coat.'

The sunshine was an unexpected bonus to a day off. They walked over Primrose Hill, with Sam admiring every dog they saw being exercised.

'I've got a dog at home,' he told Kate. 'Nice little kelpie. She's called Ripper.'

'As in 'Jack the Ripper'?'

Sam laughed. 'No. As in ripper being something extra good. Where are we going?'

'The zoo.'

'Great. And then?'

Kate laughed inwardly. So that was why Sam's attitude had seemed more casual in the last couple of days. He'd simply assumed she'd already fallen into his intended orbit. No more persuasion had been needed.

A companionable silence fell as they wandered into the zoo grounds. It wasn't broken until Sam spotted a large bronze statue of a gorilla.

'Whoa! Look at him!' Sam caught Kate's hand so she had to stop and turn. Sam seemed entranced. 'You know, he reminds me of someone.'

Kate couldn't help it. 'Tried looking in a mirror recently?'

'That does it!' Keeping a firm hold on Kate's

hand, Sam moved off briskly. 'We're going to find your mirror image now, my love. And I think we'll start in the snake-house.'

When was the last time she'd laughed so much? Kate wondered later. Much later. Come to that, when had she ever laughed so much in her life? They had stayed at the zoo until closing time at five-thirty. It had been Kate who'd insisted on ending the outing and Sam wouldn't co-operate until they'd agreed on a day's programme for her next day off.

There was really no question any more of Sam's interest in her. While Kate couldn't understand it, she felt powerless to prevent the consequences. And maybe— No, not maybe. She had to admit she wanted the consequences. Sam was so different, seemed to be so in tune with her own feelings, that it was just possible it could work. He might not ever find out what she was hiding because maybe when it came time to look it would no longer be there.

Kate hugged the thought gratefully as she went to her bookshelf. Bartholemew clambered onto her knee as she lifted her heaviest nursing manual from the bottom shelf, but she ignored him for the moment. Lifting the edges of the tissue paper beneath the book, Kate's lips curved into a gentle smile.

There it was. Perfectly flat, beautifully pressed— a single white daisy with a rather bent stem.

CHAPTER FOUR

'So you're Welsh! That explains your accent.'

'You're the one with the accent. Mine's gone. I haven't even been back there for six years.' Kate put her teacup down carefully. 'You don't really suit a tie, you know. Doesn't go with your accent.'

'Yeah! We're all savages down under.' Sam loosened the unusual item of clothing a little. 'I'm not sure it's worth it but I did always have a yen for afternoon tea at the Ritz.' He reached for the last cucumber sandwich. 'Worth it to see you wearing a dress, but don't change the subject. Why haven't you been back to Wales?'

'Nothing to go back for,' Kate replied lightly.

'What about your family?'

'It was my father's funeral I went to six years ago.'

'So you're an orphan?'

Kate hesitated. 'Not exactly. My mother's still alive.'

'But you haven't seen her for six years?'

'No.'

Sam spread a scone liberally with jam. 'Are you going to tell me why?'

'Try the clotted cream on it as well,' Kate advised. 'It's traditional. Are you going to tell me what your initials stand for?'

Sam grinned. 'Want to trade dark secrets, then?'

Kate's heart skipped a beat. For a moment she almost wanted to tell him everything, to put an end to the odd little dead-ends their conversations seemed to run into more often these days. But the fleeting desire vanished as quickly as it had come.

'Have another scone,' she offered, hoping to distract him. 'They beat the buttered crumpets hands down.'

Sam made a noncommittal noise. 'They're not bad,' he conceded. Then he leaned forward over the small table towards Kate. 'But just wait till you get out in the outback and try my damper and Cocky's joy.'

Kate's heart skipped several more beats. She was learning to welcome that wave of desire that swept through her but she did her best to look stern. 'This is a refined establishment, Dr Marshall. Try and keep it decent.'

Sam looked puzzled for less than a second. His loud guffaw made a waiter turn his head in their direction and his look was a lot sterner than Kate's.

'Cocky's joy is golden syrup,' Sam explained, 'and damper is a kind of bread you cook in the coals of an open fire or in a camp oven.' He sighed appreciatively. 'With a mug of billy tea to wash it down you'd never want a scone or clotted cream again.'

'I don't already. I've eaten far too much. I'll be useless at judo tonight.'

'Can I come and watch?'

'I thought you were doing an evening shift in Emergency.'

Sam sighed. Then he brightened. 'Where are we going tomorrow?'

'Aren't you getting tired of sightseeing? We've been almost everywhere there is in the last month.'

'Are you getting tired of showing me around?'

'No.'

'Well, then. Where are we going tomorrow?'

The changes had been so gradual that it took an accumulation before anyone really began to notice. Jeff Merrick noticed there was less formality in the way Kate spoke to patients. She smiled more often and was even heard to joke with a young man due to go to Theatre to clean up an elbow injury. They both seemed to find the checklist which queried the use of any prosthesis, false teeth or glass eyes very amusing.

Joe Millar noticed that Kate had missed her first-Monday-of-the-month haircut. The ends of her hair had started to curl. It was Margo who noticed something even more startling.

'I swear, she's wearing *make-up*,' she whispered to Jude.

'Get real! Kate?'

'Not much, but it's there. Have a look at her eyelashes. And have you noticed anything else?'

'She does seem to have been in a good mood lately.'

'Exactly. And why do you suppose that is?'

'Well, Julian's on holiday. The atmosphere around here has improved considerably.'

'True, but I think there's more to it.'

'Like what?'

'I think she's in love.'

Jude's response was modified to a conspiratorial giggle when the object of their discussion entered the resus. area.

'Haven't you two finished yet?'

'I've got to change the battery in this laryngo-scope,' Margo explained hurriedly.

'Well, get on with it. We're busy out there in case you hadn't noticed.' Kate deposited the pile of endotracheal tubes she was carrying. 'Check these balloon pumps for leakage, would you, Margo? Jude, would you clean up Mr Eder's scalp wound in cubicle three, please. Shave around it for a good inch or so. Louise is waiting to superglue it.'

Kate left the area as quickly as she'd entered. Jude raised an eyebrow. 'You were saying?'

Margo shrugged. 'I could be wrong.'

Even Kate wasn't aware of all the changes. She knew about the make-up, of course. It had taken a bit of practice to get used to it again. And she knew about missing the haircut. That appointment had been cancelled because she'd gone with Sam to see *Starlight Express* that evening and she simply hadn't got around to making another one. The heavy-duty mousse she was using was controlling it quite well enough for the moment.

Kate had no idea of how much of her personality was beginning to peep out of her shell, however. She only knew she felt happy, and that her growing friendship with Sam had added a dimension to her universe which she'd forgotten even existed.

It wasn't just the time they had together out of work hours, though there had been plenty of that in the last month. What Kate was also revelling in was the increase in enjoyment and satisfaction she gained at work. A comment or just a look from Sam that told her she'd done a good job created a glow of pleasure. Even when he was out of the department she worked with a tingle of anticipation, waiting to spot him again. She was sure no one in the department knew of their friendship or the time they spent together. Sam's friendly grin was the same for everybody.

Kate loved seeing that grin, no matter towards whom it was directed. Sam's tan had faded considerably with two months of London weather so she no longer thought about toothpaste commercials. She was still reminded of the muppets occasionally but the similarity was not derogatory. Kate had loved that television show as a child. She'd been able to guarantee it would produce a feeling of well-being and the feeling that it was, after all, a happy world she was part of. Sam's grin had the same effect now.

Julian Calder's absence for the last fortnight had been an added bonus. The unpleasant tension had been removed from her work environment and it also kept Sam a lot busier, unable to accompany his more interesting cases to Theatre or spend much time on their follow-up in the wards. He still managed several times to visit the patient to whom he'd applied the external pelvic fixation, and he was always keen to share knowledge of progress with anyone interested.

Kate normally had little opportunity or time to find out about their cases after they'd left the emergency department. It added surprisingly to the feeling that their brief contact with patients was worthwhile in more than just physical terms. People often remembered with deep gratitude the comfort and reassurance they received initially. Kate found real pleasure in learning more about them and their outcomes. As Sam's enthusiasm became known people went out of their way to keep him informed. They appreciated his interest and, like Kate, were becoming increasingly impressed by his skills.

She watched him later that afternoon as he inserted a second chest drain in a road-accident victim. The incision parallel to the ribs was swift, the dissection of the intercostal muscles confident. As Sam slipped a gloved finger into the chest to check for any adhesions Kate was struck, not for the first time, by what delicate and controlled movements those large hands were capable of. She was ready with the intercostal drainage tube and a haemostat as soon as Sam glanced up. She then connected the tubing to the underwater-seal drain and they both watched the rise and fall of the water level in the drainage bottle as their patient breathed.

Sam nodded. 'Good. We're in the thoracic cavity. I'll have a suture, thanks, Katy.'

Katy. No one ever called her that. Her father had but only until she was about five. Peter had tried once but at eighteen Kate had been far too mature to consider it acceptable. No one would have dared in the last ten years. Only Sam, and Kate found, to her surprise, that she liked it.

'We'd better have another chest X-ray.'

Kate stepped away from the bed. She watched Sam's face as he pondered the monitors. He was still not happy with his patient's condition.

'We've still got major blood loss somewhere,' he murmured to Kate.

They were standing side by side—so close that their hips were touching. Kate could feel the electricity being generated. She could feel it even without the contact. Why couldn't Sam? The hand-holding had become almost routine after that first day at the zoo. Kate had expected more after the visits to Westminster Abbey and Madame Tussaud's. He had kissed her for the first time during their tour of the Tower of London—a brief, soft caress which had still been enough to leave Kate shaky at the knees. The gentle kiss was now as routine as the hand-holding, but Kate had barely noticed the changing of the guard at Buckingham Palace last weekend.

The desire to have Sam touch her was almost overwhelming, but he seemed so relaxed, seemed to want only her company and conversation. Their friendship was wonderful but it was no longer enough for Kate. She needed him to want more. This time, Kate felt certain, she would be able to respond.

'Kate?'

'Sorry?' Kate jumped guiltily. The X-ray technicians were moving their equipment away.

'We're going to do a peritoneal lavage. We'll need to aspirate the stomach contents first. Are you set up?'

'Of course.' Kate dismissed the personal train of thought without hesitation. She handed Sam an orogastric tube and large syringe, then helped Louise as she inserted a urinary catheter. Roger surveyed the scene from behind the ventilating equipment.

'This guy's beginning to look like a packet of straws,' he commented wryly.

'We're not finished yet.' Sam filled the syringe attached to the orogastric tube for the fourth time. 'That's about it for here. Have we got his bladder empty?'

Kate checked the length of tubing as she taped the drainage bag to the side of the bed. 'Yes,' she reported. 'Nearly 200 ml out so it was pretty full.'

'Probably pure alcohol,' Sam muttered. 'Like his stomach contents. Nobody light a match! I'm surprised he could even keep his balance on that bike, let alone get it out on the motorway.' Sam moved to the sink and stripped off his gloves, holding his hands under the soap dispenser. 'Let's have a ten-degree head-down tilt,' he advised Roger, taking a sterile towel from the pack Joe ripped open for him.

Kate had already covered the patient's abdomen with green sterile drapes and painted the skin with antiseptic. Sam took a scalpel and made a small longitudinal midline incision below the umbilicus.

'Hold these artery forceps for me, Kate,' he instructed a minute later. 'I'm going to make the incision into the peritoneum.'

With the peritoneal dialysis catheter in place, Sam attached a syringe and gently aspirated the catheter.

'Negative,' he commented. 'Have you warmed the saline, Joe?'

'All set.'

They began to run a litre of the fluid into the catheter through an IV set.

'Look at that!' Sam was pointing to the bottle connected to the chest drain. A trickle of clear fluid had begun.

'We've got a diaphragmatic rupture. Right, let's cut the lavage and get this guy up to Theatre.'

It was a long day, made even longer by the new tension Kate was experiencing. Frustration. And nervousness. Kate was nervous because she was quite sure that Sam must know how she felt. He couldn't be so tuned in to everything else and have missed something her body was now shouting. Perhaps it was because the desire was purely one-sided.

The realisation that it wasn't came to her quite suddenly that afternoon. The brush of his fingers on her hand as she'd handed him a pack of sterile dressings had seemed accidental. It probably had been, and it would have been meaningless had it not been for the look that followed the contact. No one else could have read anything into that brief second of eye contact but Kate could. The message was as clear as if it had been spoken. Sam was waiting for a signal from her—one she knew she was ready to give.

Louise Grant handed a patient's chart to Kate as she was leaving the department after her shift. The registrar looked harassed.

'Could you do me a favour and drop that on Jeff's desk, please, Kate? It's the Dead on Arrival we had with suspicious circumstances. The police want a word with the head of department first thing in the morning and it'll get buried if I leave it here any longer.'

'Sure.' Kate looked around. The place was humming, the rest of the day shift looking relieved as they escaped the pressure. She wondered if she should offer to stay on but dismissed the thought. Kate wanted to catch Sam and invite him home for a meal. He hadn't been inside her flat since the night she'd flattened him. If any signal was needed she knew that was it. But Sam was not to be seen in the department and Kate felt even more frustrated as she ran lightly up the stairs to the consultants' offices. He must have left earlier.

The wave of relief she felt on finding Sam in Jeff Merrick's office made Kate catch her breath.

'I thought you'd gone already.'

'Had some paperwork to catch up on. Were you looking for me, Katy?'

Kate put the chart on the desk. 'I was just bringing this in but, seeing as you're here, would you like to risk my cooking and have dinner at my place?' The words came out in a rush and Kate could feel the tension as Sam hesitated and rose from the desk. The signal had been given. What was the response going to be?

He moved until he was standing very close to Kate. 'I'd like that,' he said slowly. 'I'd really like that, but I've promised the crew I'd meet them at the pub. There's a drinks session on for Margo's birthday.'

'Oh, of course. I'd forgotten.' Kate knew she sounded flustered. Did he know she hadn't been invited?

'Why don't you come to the pub?'

'No. I'd rather not.' Kate bit her lip. 'I mean, I wanted…'

The gap narrowed between them as Sam's fingers closed gently under Kate's chin. 'I know,' he said softly. 'Me, too.' He tilted her chin as he bent his head and his lips touched hers.

Kate's lips opened as she gasped. This was not the gentle caress she was accustomed to. She could feel the power of Sam's desire as his lips pressed more firmly and moved over hers. Her own desire rose to meet it. Instinctively she moved her hands up onto his shoulders and then around his neck as she was drawn closer. Sam's hands moved down her back, pressing her against his chest, and she felt his tongue sweep her own. Sam's hands felt heavier, the pressure building. The power of desire was enclosing them, uncontrollable. Kate stiffened but was pressed too close to Sam's body. She couldn't move—couldn't breathe!

Desperately Kate turned her head to break the contact between their lips. She wrenched herself out of his arms, stumbling in her haste to step back. He ignored the door that had opened behind her.

'Katy? What's wrong? You look like you've seen a ghost.'

Kate's breath came in short gasps. She was struggling to control it as Louise spoke. 'Thank goodness you're still here, Sam. Could you spare a few minutes?' She didn't seem to notice Kate. 'We're already stretched and we've got an RTA and a stabbing victim on the way in.'

'On my way.' Sam paused only briefly to look carefully at Kate. 'Are you all right?'

'I'm fine,' Kate lied. 'I got a fright when the door opened.'

She hadn't convinced Sam. 'We'll talk later,' he promised. 'I'll ring you.'

The ringing of the phone was horribly persistent. Kate had to fight the urge to pick it up and leave it off the hook, but then he'd know she was at home, and it would be just like him to turn up on the doorstep—even if it was the middle of the night. It was the third time it had rung. Surely, now he would give up.

Kate hunched further under the patchwork quilt. She didn't close her eyes. The kiss wouldn't go away and if she made it dark the turmoil simply spiralled into nightmare.

That feeling of power—of desire. It was how it

had started. It had been exactly the same with Peter, but Kate had not been ready and her own desire had fled at his insistence.

'We're practically engaged, Kate. Don't be such a prude.'

'No.'

'Girls always say no. They're supposed to. You really mean yes. You'll see, you'll like it.'

The flashes of memory. The smell of alcohol, the physical pain, the humiliation. 'What's wrong with you, Kate? Are you frigid or something?'

The phone rang again. Kate pulled the pillow over her head and muffled the sound. The darkness was suffocating. Kate felt the tears escape again as she pushed the pillow away.

Why wouldn't the fear ever go away? It wasn't a fear of physical pain. Kate knew that wasn't the problem. It was the betrayal. And not just from Peter. The voice of her best friend, Elizabeth, jangled in her memory.

'What did you expect, Kate? His parents were away and you went home with him. Who's still a virgin when they're eighteen anyway? What's wrong with you?'

Even her mother. Especially her mother.

'Peter's going into his father's law firm. He's got a good future. What can you possibly achieve with an accusation like this? What's wrong with you, Kate? For goodness' sake, can't you even consider your own reputation? What would people *think*?

'Are you pregnant, Kate? Is that what you're trying to tell me? Did you think it might be more acceptable if you pretended you hadn't wanted it? What is it that you *do* want?'

It had been years before Kate had really under-stood what she'd wanted in the mute agony of those days, years of living away from home as she'd com-pleted her nursing training in the unfamiliar Northern city she'd chosen to flee to.

She'd wanted to know that that wasn't what it was supposed to have been like. She'd wanted to know that she could trust someone she loved not to hurt her. She'd just wanted someone to hold her and tell her that everything was going to be all right. The betrayal of her body had been by Peter, but he hadn't been the only one to betray her trust and love. Her best friend had contributed. And her mother had taken first prize.

The conviction that there was, in fact, something wrong with her had taken root. The satisfaction gained from her early nursing career had almost con-vinced her otherwise. Her friendships had been cau-tious but had grown. Then there had been James. Everybody had liked James. Kate was so lucky to be the one he'd picked to date. But James had also wanted too much too soon. Her friends hadn't un-derstood her reluctance and James's frustration had finally been turned against her.

'I can't be bothered, being mucked about like this, Kate. What's wrong with you?'

Kate knew. She now knew what was wrong with her. It was just lucky it didn't show on the outside like other physical disabilities. A move to London, self-defence classes, a new job and a new image—a new life in which she could accept what she'd never have.

Now that acceptance had gone—blown away by her desire for a man who was only going to be in

her life for a few short months anyway. She wanted
him so desperately, wanted his friendship, his love
and…his touch. She wanted it to the point of physical pain but knew what would happen when he
found out she couldn't respond. She had learned to
live with betrayal in the past but this was something
else, something so powerful she had thought it would
be enough to change the past. To heal her. The realisation that it wasn't was unbearable.

She hadn't cried since her father's funeral. It felt
like another death now.

'Kate, you look awful! Are you ill?'
    'No. You know me, Margo. I'm never ill.'
    'Well, you don't look too good this morning.'
    'I'm fine. Not enough sleep, I guess.'
    In fact, she'd had no sleep at all. Only the fact that
she had three days off, starting tomorrow, had per-
suaded Kate not to call in sick today. She could make
it through one day. The distraction of throwing herself into other people's problems could only help. It
was a strategy that had worked before and it did
again now, and by the time Kate was seeing her third
patient she felt on top of things, and by the time she
encountered Sam by the whiteboard she knew she
could cope. For once, Sam's grin was absent.
    'Are you all right, Katy? I was worried about you.'
    'Were you? I'm fine, thanks. Could you look at
Mrs Jessop in cubicle one? She's ninety-two. Her
daughter found her this morning. Looks like a
stroke.'
    'Why didn't you answer the phone?'
    'Didn't I?' Kate scooped up the blood samples

she'd left on the desk. 'I can't have heard it. Perhaps I had the headphones on, listening to some music.'

Sam just looked at her. Kate wasn't used to telling lies. She knew her cheeks had reddened.

'Cubicle one, you said?'

'That's right. Thanks.'

It was easy to cope while the department was busy. The problem came when it hit a sudden lull mid-afternoon. Kate was more than due for a break and needed to avoid the laughter and good humour, emanating from the common room. She slipped outside and hurried over to the park.

'You can't accuse me of following you this time.'

'No.' Kate joined Sam on his bench. There was really no way of avoiding it. Out of the frying pan and into the fire, she thought ruefully.

Sam took hold of her hand but Kate avoided his eye. 'Julian's back tomorrow. I thought I could take a couple of days off. I'd rather like to see a bit of Cornwall. Come away with me, Katy?'

'I can't,' Kate said quickly. 'I've got no one to look after Bartholemew.'

'What do you do when you go backpacking through the wilds of Turkey, then?'

Kate was silent. There was no way out of that one.

'So, if it's not the cat,' Sam persisted, 'why can't you come away with me?'

Kate chewed at her lip. 'It would change things,' she said finally.

Sam stroked the hand he held. 'Things have already changed, Kate. Hadn't you noticed?'

Kate nodded. She could sense Sam watching her closely. Too closely.

'I thought Louise, coming into the office like that

last night, had given you a fright. It was more than that, though, wasn't it?'

Kate still couldn't meet his gaze. She had one card left to try, one chance left to hang onto what she had with this man. 'I don't want things to change,' she said quietly. 'I like what we had.'

'Me, too. But "had" is the operative word there. I don't want to keep sightseeing around London for ever. Your company means a bit more to me than a tour guide. You asked me to dinner last night. You wanted that kiss as much as I did.' Sam squeezed her hand more firmly. 'So, what's made you change your mind?'

'I haven't,' Kate protested.

'Don't play games, Katy. We're both old enough to know better.' Sam dropped her hand and instead used his forefinger to turn Kate's chin. She was forced to look at him. 'Talk to me,' he ordered unsmilingly.

Kate knew she'd lost. She'd always known he could see too much.

'There's no point in going on, Sam. I can't give you what you want.'

'What is it that I want?'

'A—a relationship,' Kate stammered.

'We already have a relationship.' Sam wasn't going to help her. 'Rather a good one, in my opinion. I'm in love with you, Kate Campbell. Or hadn't you noticed?'

'But it's not that sort of relationship,' Kate said desperately. 'We haven't... We're not—'

'Lovers?' Sam supplied calmly. 'No. Not yet. I think it might be something that we both want, though. Come away with me for a couple of days and let's find out.'

'No! I can't!'

'Why? Why not, Kate?'

There was a moment of heavy silence, then Sam sighed wearily. 'Doesn't our friendship mean anything to you, Kate?'

'Of course it does. A lot.'

'Then doesn't it at least deserve some honesty?'

Kate finally met his gaze again. The intensity of it only added to her pain. It had to be ended, for both their sakes.

'I can't go to bed with you, Sam. Not ever. So don't waste any more of your time. You'll only be disappointed.'

'You mean you don't want to go to bed with me?'

'Yes. No— I mean, I can't.'

'Why not?'

'Because I can't.' Kate looked away from his burning gaze. 'There's something wrong with me, Sam. I'm...I'm frigid.' It was the first time Kate had ever used the word aloud, though she'd heard it often enough in her mind ever since Peter's accusation. She only whispered it now but it seemed to echo loudly in the short silence that followed.

'Bullshit!' Sam informed her. His vehemence startled Kate. 'That's absolute rubbish, Kate. Why do you even say it?'

'I don't want to talk about it. It's time I got back to work.' Kate tried to stand but Sam caught her hand and pulled her back onto the bench.

'This is more important. I want to know why you said that.'

'Leave me alone, Sam. Please!'

This time Sam allowed her to stand. 'Fine,' he said heavily. 'If that's what you want, Kate. You run away and I'll leave you alone. But your excuse is pretty damned lousy.'

Kate was already walking away. Sam raised his voice to make sure she could still hear him.

'And what's more, I don't believe it!'

CHAPTER FIVE

IT WAS like a scene from the depths of hell.

Resus. one looked as if a massacre had taken place there. The paramedic staff were white-faced and covered with blood.

'Watch out for glass!' they kept repeating as they transferred their charge.

Blood, glass, too many voices, all speaking at once. The victim was a young female but she would now be unrecognisable to any who knew her. The horrific facial injuries had obliterated her features, the heavy bleeding soaking through the long blonde hair that fell over the edges of the pillow. Jeff Merrick and Sam were attempting to insert an airway. Even Kate had to look away. Margo's hands were shaking noticeably as she tried to attach ECG electrodes.

Joe's gloved hands were blood-covered, his face grim as he attempted to continue the cardiac compressions the paramedics had begun. Kate tried to ignore it as she concentrated on her own task. A shower of glass landed in the puddles of blood as she cut away what was left of the woman's dress, exposing a grossly distended abdomen.

'Twelve-gauge needle-cannula,' she heard Sam order. 'Get a Y-connector on the oxygen supply.'

'No output, no BP.' Margo had an edge of panic in her voice.

Kate tore the stethoscope away from her ears. 'I've

got a foetal heartbeat,' she called excitedly. 'One-twenty—dropping to one-ten.'

'What gestation do you think?' Jeff Merrick was beside her.

'I'd guess between thirty and thirty-four weeks.'

'Is the husband conscious?'

'Not yet. Julian's got him.'

'Still no output.' Margo was staring at the young mother's face with an expression of horror.

'I'm going for a thoracotamy,' Sam said grimly. 'Jeff?'

The emergency department director nodded, his face equally grim. Joe stopped his cardiac massage and moved aside as Sam took up a scalpel.

Kate caught Jeff's eye. The internal cardiac massage was not going to save the woman but might buy them a little time. Jeff reached for another scalpel from the trolley Kate had placed nearby.

'Someone get paediatrics here, stat.'

More staff flowed into the area and even the most experienced gasped at the scene. The woman's chest was opened, metallic rib-spreaders framing Sam's hands as he held the heart and squeezed rhythmically. Her belly was also opened with a sweeping vertical incision. The bleeding was minimal, the circulation shut down despite Sam's desperate efforts.

Kate held her breath as she handed Jeff the surgical scissors to cut the uterine membranes. She watched his face as he slipped his hand inside and knew from his expression when he had located the baby's head. He took the obstetric forceps from her with his other hand. It had taken less than two minutes to deliver the baby. The tiny, limp body was rushed to the next bed in the resus. area just as the paediatric team arrived, the registrar wheeling an incubator at a run.

Kate saw the nod that passed between the consultants at the mother's side. There was no point in continuing any efforts at resuscitation. From the glimpses Kate caught of the baby, now lying beneath the heat of a radiant warmer as the paediatricians began their own resuscitation attempts, it didn't look good. The bag and mask ventilation continued as ECG leads were attached and IV access gained. The tiny form still looked lifeless.

'We'll intubate,' she heard someone say.

Margo was in tears, her hands shaking too much to release the rib-spreaders she was trying to remove. Kate put her arm around the young nurse's shoulders.

'I'll do that,' she said. 'Get a clean gown on and go and have a coffee. When you're ready you can see if Julian needs any help with the baby's father. We've still got the other driver to see to as well.'

'He can wait.'

Kate glanced up sharply at Sam's bitter tone but said nothing. The heavily intoxicated youth had been placed in a cubicle, suffering from little more than lacerations and a suspected broken ankle. His loud and abusive demands for attention could be heard whenever the resus. doors swung open as staff and equipment circulated. She heard him again now as Sam walked out.

Joe gathered the last of the surgical instruments, piling them onto a trolley and throwing a drape over the top to conceal the tangled heap of bloodstained steel. Kate helped him draw a clean white sheet over the woman's body and found she was biting her lip hard. She didn't even know the woman's name.

'Five-minute Apgar score of two,' the paediatric registrar called. Kate's heart sank a little further.

'Looks like I missed all the excitement.' Julian Calder sounded disappointed as he began to draw back the sheet on the bed beside Kate.

'Don't do that,' she snapped.

Julian raised his eyebrows. 'I beg your pardon?'

'There's nothing more we can do for her,' Kate said defensively. 'She doesn't need to become a side-show.'

Julian said nothing but she held his stare for what seemed a long time. The tense moment was broken by the reappearance of Sam.

'The X-rays are through on Ray Donnelly,' he told Julian. 'Six fractured ribs but no skull fracture.'

'Pretty severe concussion.' Julian dropped the edge of the sheet he was still holding. 'He'll still need a CT scan and observation for a while.'

'Has he been told about his wife?'

'Not yet. I just came in to find out what had happened.'

Sam shook his head. 'Horrific injuries. We didn't stand a chance. I'm amazed the baby survived.'

'How's it doing?'

The consultants both moved towards the next bed. The baby was being transferred to the double-walled incubator.

'We'll get her upstairs,' the paediatrician told them. 'She's stable. I'd give her about a fifty per cent chance right now. Do you know what gestation she is?'

'Thirty-four weeks today. The husband was driving the mother in to an antenatal check-up.'

The paediatrician shook his head. 'Any other children?'

'This is their first. They've only been married for a year. He's twenty-two. She was only twenty.' Even Julian was looking shaken by the tragedy. 'The juvenile delinquent that ran into them head-on is sixteen. Doesn't even have a driver's licence and the car was stolen.'

Kate watched the paediatric team wheel their tiny cargo from the area. A heavy silence fell as Sam and Julian also left.

Joe caught Kate's eye. 'I'll finish cleaning up here,' he offered.

'Thanks, Joe. I'd better see if Margo's OK.' She hesitated a moment. 'Doesn't get much more gruesome than that, does it?'

'At least we saved the baby,' Joe said quietly. 'Not the best one to walk in on after three days off, though. Are you all right?'

'Of course. Aren't I always?' Kate's expression was as blank as her tone. Moving towards the common room, Kate could hear anguished wailing from a cubicle, and knew that Julian or Sam had told Ray Donnelly about his wife. She winced visibly at the pain and disbelief being expressed, and hoped the other staff were coping better than Margo whom she told to stay put in the common room for a while.

Kate took a deep breath as she entered cubicle five. Shane Burrell was the youth who had caused the Donnellys' accident. As unpleasant as the duty was, he still required the same professional treatment as his victims.

'About bloody time,' he greeted her. 'Where's the

doctor? I haven't even had anything for the bloody pain!'

'There have been people more seriously injured than you, Mr Burrell. A doctor will be in to see you shortly.'

'There'd better be. I want my ankle fixed up. I don't give a stuff about the other people.'

No, Kate thought. You obviously don't give a stuff. An image of the sheeted woman whose name she still didn't know made Kate blink hard. She picked up a pair of scissors.

'I'm going to have to cut your jeans and get that boot off so we can X-ray this ankle.'

'Don't you bloody touch my jeans.' The youth sat up aggressively. Kate was almost overpowered by the smell of alcohol as his shaven head loomed closer to hers. She found the scissors wrenched from her hand and turned so that the blades were facing her. In the stunned moment before she could react Kate heard the curtain of the cubicle being pulled roughly open. Thank God, she thought, and turned to see what staff member had arrived in time to help. But it wasn't a staff member. The young man was wearing a hospital gown. He held one arm against his chest and was breathing in painful gasps.

'You bastard!' he shouted. 'You killed Jessie.' His voice was racked with sobs and painful groaning. 'Do you have any idea at all what you've done?'

The man swayed and lurched sideways into Julian Calder's grip. Sam had materialised at the same time and his look was murderous as he advanced on Shane Burrell, now climbing off his bed with the scissors still menacingly pointed outwards.

Jessie. Her name was Jessie. Kate watched as Joe

helped Julian support Ray Donnelly and lead him away. She watched Sam grab Shane's arm and twist it backwards until the scissors clattered to the floor.

'He was going to hit me,' whined the youth. 'I was only protecting myself.'

Sam pushed him flat none too gently. 'You're lucky I don't hit you myself,' he snapped.

Kate collected the scissors. 'Shall I call Security?'

'Good idea. I think we'll have to wait to treat Mr Burrell here until they arrive.'

'What about pain relief?'

Sam's voice was cold. 'That can wait as well.'

Kate followed Sam from the cubicle. 'We really should give him some analgesia,' she said quietly.

Sam turned his head. He still looked furious. 'I'll see to it in a minute,' he said tersely, 'when I've stopped feeling like murdering the little bastard.' He smiled without mirth. 'Shocked at my unprofessional attitude, are you, Kate?' He stopped walking and gripped her arm. 'Why don't you show what you feel, Kate Campbell? You're allowed to be human occasionally as well, you know.'

The tension of the day seemed to feed on itself. Small incidents, normally overlooked, assumed unusual proportions. Kate saw Julian, obviously chatting up the new student nurse, Bonnie, who looked flustered. She moved in.

'Bonnie, go and see Joe in cubicle two. He's setting up an infusion for a little boy with asthma. You may be able to help.'

Julian said nothing as he watched the girl leave hurriedly. He moved over to where Margo was setting up a trolley and Kate saw his hand close over the nurse's as he whispered something in her ear.

Margo stepped to one side and pulled her hand clear as Kate appeared beside her. It was Kate's turn to say nothing, but she met Julian's gaze challengingly. With a silent whistle the junior consultant moved away.

'You don't have to put up with it, you know,' Kate told Margo. She didn't care if Julian could hear her. In fact, she hoped he could. 'We've got enough to deal with around here without harassment. Let me know if it's a problem.'

Was it just because he had been absent for a fortnight that Julian Calder's behaviour seemed so obnoxious? Or was it that the traumatic start to the day's duties had unsettled the whole department? Maybe it was because Kate's own defences were being eroded. The edges of her carefully built universe were crumbling, and as yet she had no clues as to how to begin rebuilding.

The day got worse. Even a break for a cup of tea after lunch in a peaceful common room didn't help Kate. She had decided to avoid the park because she didn't want the possibility of finding herself alone with Sam. When he entered the common room at the same time as Joe and Margo left, Kate decided she couldn't win. After a minute's uncomfortable silence she made an attempt at conversation.

'How was Cornwall?'

'Great.' Sam was spooning coffee into a mug. 'Could have been better, but…'

'Was the weather bad?'

Sam shrugged. 'You could say it was dampened a bit. But not by the weather.' He sipped at his drink.

'Oh?' Kate felt uneasy under the serious scrutiny she was receiving. She looked away. Surely someone else would come in for a break before things got any heavier, but the door remained closed.

'It's kind of like the volume knob's turned down on everything when you haven't got anyone special to share it with,' Sam told her musingly. 'The scenery isn't as beautiful, the colours aren't as bright. The adventure's not as exciting. Even the food doesn't taste as good. And the memories, well, they're sort of hollow. Kind of 2-D instead of 3-D.' His voice deepened. 'I missed you, Kate.'

Kate kept her head bent. She'd missed Sam more than she'd thought possible. She'd hoped desperately that he'd given up on going away and would suddenly turn up on her doorstep. Hoped and dreaded it at the same time.

In an effort to distract herself Kate had reread her travel journals and pored over the brochures for the holiday she was planning in Africa. But the appeal of both the past and especially the future trips had mysteriously gone. Sam had just put his finger on the reason. To do things alone removed a dimension from the experience, and to do things without Sam now seemed hardly worth the consideration. Kate could almost feel another large chunk of her defence crumble. She'd known that letting someone into her life had been a mistake, had known that sharing her secret could be enough to destroy her. Now she felt helpless to prevent the inevitable.

Kate almost bumped into Julian as she fled the common room, after excusing herself hurriedly.

'Do some obs on cubicle three some time in the next half-hour,' Julian instructed. 'Got a forty-three-year-old woman with abdominal pain.'

'Possible appendicitis?' Kate enquired. She knew her tone held more than an edge of sarcasm.

'Could be,' Julian agreed. 'Or maybe just constipation. I'll have another look when I've had a coffee.'

'Not all abdominal pain is appendicitis,' Kate snapped. 'Or constipation. And things like ruptured ectopic pregnancies don't do very well when you put them on hold for hours.'

Julian's eyes narrowed. 'I don't know what's come over you while I've been away, Kate, but I can't say I'm too impressed.' He moved closer to her. Too close, but Kate didn't back away. 'Just watch your own performance very carefully from now on, Nurse Campbell,' he said softly, 'because that's exactly what I'll be doing.'

The impact of the Donnelly tragedy seemed to hang over the department for days. Professionally the teamwork was as good as ever and the more serious cases and other tragedies came and went. It was the atmosphere which had changed. It was as though a black cloud had settled over the emergency department of St Matthew's and everyone was waiting for the storm to break.

Jeff called Kate and Joe to his office.

'What's going on?' he queried with a frown. 'Has something happened that I don't know about?'

'Only the usual hassles,' Kate replied. 'Staff shortages, uncooperative patients, beds not available when we need them...'

Joe nodded his agreement. 'Tempers get frayed. The talk of management cuts in staff numbers and the equipment budget doesn't help. It makes it seem less likely that we'll be successful in finally setting up our flying squad. That's going to disappoint a few people.'

Kate nodded. The department had been fighting to establish a flying squad for over a year now. The benefits of having a fully qualified medical team available to attend major accidents was well recognised. The first hour following serious injury—the 'golden hour'—was the most critical. It was the time when deaths occurred from heavy bleeding or breathing difficulties which could often have been prevented by appropriate and skilled intervention—and flying squads were the most effective way of treating people within that time frame. Both Kate and Joe were desperately keen to be involved, but talk of funding cuts had dashed their current hopes. However, Jeff didn't look convinced.

'Margo's been distressed ever since the post-mortem Caesar on Mrs Donnelly,' Kate added. 'And our new student doesn't seem to be coping. I've found her in tears more than once.'

Jeff Merrick nodded wearily. 'I know, but the department usually rises above this sort of thing. Something's changed in the last week and it bothers me. Even Sam doesn't look too happy. The only thing I can think of is that Julian's back from holiday.'

Kate and Joe exchanged a quick glance but said nothing.

Jeff sighed. 'Julian's only ever seen emergency work as a stepping-stone. He was very confident of getting the intensive care consultancy he went for last year. Too confident. He does a good job in the more serious cases but I know his attitude to the bulk of the workload leaves a lot to be desired. I've been hoping he'd get over it but I'm beginning to wonder if his attitude is affecting others.' He looked directly at Kate. 'I just happened to do a case review on a young woman last week, a case of Julian's that seemed to be in the department for quite some time before a ruptured ectopic pregnancy was diagnosed.'

Kate met the direct look. 'The department was busy,' she said cautiously. 'The outcome was successful.'

'This time,' Jeff said. 'In future I'd like incidents like that brought to my attention. I'm wondering how many more there are that I don't know about.'

Kate and Joe left the office, feeling subdued. They both paused at the top of the stairs and looked over the bannister at the activity below. Wheelchairs and trolleys rolled past, a man was banging on a drinks dispenser that wasn't performing and Patsy was having an altercation with another man who was waving a bloodstained bandaged thumb under her nose. Joe sighed heavily.

'I'm beginning to think it's time for a change.'

'Oh, Joe. You've been here as long as I have. We're part of the furniture.'

'Quite. Maybe I've got burn-out.'

'It's just a bad week. Things will improve.'

'I doubt it.'

Kate glanced up at his tone. 'What's wrong, Joe?'

'I was out last night—at a nightclub. With my partner.'

'So?'

'So Julian Calder was at the same club.'

'Oh.' Kate tried to give her colleague an encour-

aging smile. 'Julian's been on my case for months.
You get used to it.'

Joe snorted. 'What kind of attitude is that, Kate?
And, anyway, you don't look too happy yourself
these days.'

Kate had no response to that. She waved a hand
at the scene below them. 'Come on. Back to the salt
mines.'

The low point of the week for Kate came the following morning. They all heard the screams for help as
the anguished woman ran into the emergency department. Kate took the baby from her arms and others tried to calm the mother as they led her to a
private waiting room. Sam and Louise were already
in the resus. area as Kate ran in, but there was nothing they could do. The baby was already dead. The
mother's frantic attempts at CPR even as she'd run
for help had been pointless. The six-week-old baby
boy was cold and must have died during the night
as he slept.

It was Kate who carried the tiny bundle to a side-
room. The mother would be brought in shortly to
spend some time with her infant before the other
necessary arrangements were carried out. Kate re-
buttoned the blue stretch-suit and arranged the hand-
knitted shawl around the tiny face. The baby's eyes
were shut, the lips opened and curved almost in a
smile. Kate stroked a downy cheek with her finger.
Alone in the private and dimly lit room, Kate pressed
her hands to her face and her shoulders heaved in
silent sobs.

The door opened quietly behind her and then
closed again.

'Are you ready for me to bring in Michael's mum?'

Kate shook her head. A stifled sob escaped her lips.

'Oh, Katy,' Sam whispered. She felt his arm around her shoulders and turned her head to rest against him.

'It's not fair, is it?' he murmured. 'A life taken away before it's even begun.' He tightened his hold on Kate. 'I went to see Ray Donnelly this morning. He's going to be discharged. The baby's doing very well. He's called her Hope.'

Kate reached for the box of tissues she'd placed on the end of the bed. She blew her nose.

'I guess that's what she is,' Sam continued quietly. 'His hope for the future.'

Sam also took a tissue from the box. He wiped the tears that still trickled down Kate's cheeks. 'We all need that, Katy. Wee Michael here can't choose, but you can. Don't throw your life away.'

'I'm not,' Kate said brokenly. 'I've only ever tried to put it back together.'

The clear blue eyes were steady on hers. 'Someone's hurt you, Katy. Done as much damage as that drunken idiot did to Ray Donnelly. Maybe you'll never be able to tell me about it but I'd like to deal with the bastard as much as I'd like to have sorted out Shane Burrell. People like that don't deserve to win. Don't let them.'

Sam bent suddenly and kissed Kate softly. He used his thumb to wipe away the final dampness on her cheek. 'We only get one shot at life, Kate. There's no dress rehearsal.' His gaze went back to the tiny bundle on the bed beside them. 'We see too much evidence of that every day.'

Kate could see the glint of tears in Sam's eyes as she turned away. 'I'm going to bring Michael's mother in now,' he told her softly. 'Do you want to stay?'

Kate swallowed hard. 'I'll cope,' she said, more confidently than she felt.

'I'll be here too, remember.' Sam's gaze was as gentle as his voice. 'You don't have to cope alone.'

CHAPTER SIX

'HAVE you seen Jeff?'

Sam looked up from the hand he was examining. 'He's in a meeting with management. Looks like your flying squad might become a reality. Should be back by about nine.'

'OK.' Kate hesitated. 'Could you sign these requisition forms for me? It's not that urgent but it will be later if the pace keeps up like this.'

'Sure.' Sam took the pen and scribbled his signature at the points Kate indicated. 'Amazing how many people can injure themselves by breakfast-time.' He grinned over his shoulder at his patient. 'Max here decided to repair the loose floorboard in his kitchen.'

'Only I missed the nail and got my thumb.' The burly man held out his hand towards Kate. The tip of his thumb was grossly swollen, the nail already completely black. 'It's killing me, Doc. Can't you do something?'

'We'll sort it out now, mate. At least we know it's not broken.' He handed the forms back to Kate. 'Can you find me a paper-clip? A metal one.'

'I'll look after the papers.'

'No, *I* want one.'

'Why?'

'Just do it, Kate. Don't argue about it.'

Kate's eyes widened at his tone. It was the closest she'd ever heard Sam come to snapping at anyone.

Was it just the pressure of an overly busy start to the day? The atmosphere in the department seemed to have settled in the last couple of days. She'd even thought that she and Sam might be re-establishing their friendship since the distressing case of baby Michael. Turning to leave, she was relieved to hear Sam's tone lighten.

'Have you got a cigarette lighter on you, Kate?'

'Of course.' Kate managed a grin. 'I'm a chain-smoker. Haven't you noticed?'

Sam didn't return her smile. 'Some people are very good at hiding things, Kate.'

Kate winced inwardly. Barbed comments from Julian could be expected and brushed off, but one from Sam hurt. It hurt a lot.

'I've got a lighter, Doc.' Max fished in his jeans pocket with his good hand. 'Would you like a smoke, too?'

'Not just now, ta.' Sam was grinning again. 'I'll just go and find the rest of my surgical equipment.'

He followed Kate as she moved to the central desk. She deposited her requisition forms into the internal mail system, scanning the desk as she did so.

'These clips seem to be all plastic.'

'Hmm. No good.' Sam's gaze was directed towards Joe and the X-rays he was examining on the monitors. 'No fracture on Mrs Fife's ankle there, Joe. Just needs strapping. What's this one?'

'This guy's wife was backing out of their drive-way. Ran over his foot. Julian saw him.'

'Has he seen the X-ray?'

'Not yet.'

'Not much we can do. Strap the broken toe to the

one beside it and advise him to wear a firm-soled shoe. It's going to be painful for a while, give him some painkillers to take home. Let's get some of these cubicles clear.'

'Found one!' Kate triumphantly held up a metal paper-clip.

'Great.' Sam nodded. 'Where's Julian at the moment?'

Joe emerged from the supply room with some crêpe bandages in his hand. 'Maybe there's nothing serious enough to interest him just yet,' he said with a wry smile.

The curtain in cubicle four, the nearest to the desk, slid open suddenly as Joe spoke and Julian appeared beside him.

'We all know what interests you, though, don't we, Joe?'

The momentary silence was sinister. Kate could feel all the tension of the last week crowding back around them. Suddenly she felt angry.

'Drop it, Julian.'

Julian raised his eyebrow in Kate's direction. 'Sticking together, are we?' He smiled knowingly. 'Takes one to know one, I suppose.'

Sam reached over and took the paper-clip Kate was still holding up. 'Let's just get on with the job, eh?'

Julian shrugged. He turned his gaze from Kate to the whiteboard. 'What's in two, then?'

'Woman who's convinced she swallowed a fishbone at breakfast. I haven't had time to see her. Louise was going to after she's finished suturing the laceration in three.'

'I'll have a look,' Julian offered. 'Tell Joe to get me a laryngoscope.'

'He's busy,' Kate told him.

'Well, you get it, then.'

'Kate's coming with me. Why don't you get it yourself, Julian?'

Kate followed Sam at a trot. 'That's not like you, Sam.'

'What's not?'

'Snapping at people. Being unfriendly.'

'Maybe being friends isn't all it's cracked up to be. Maybe I'm fed up with this place and the way people won't stand up for themselves.' He drew the curtain back sharply.

'I'm not going to let Julian hassle Joe.' Kate turned to smile at Max who was gripping the wrist of his injured hand, his face twisted with pain.

Sam straightened out the paper-clip. 'Julian's not really your biggest problem, though, is he, Kate?' He flicked the cigarette lighter and held the tip of the paper-clip into the flame. 'Now, let's get on with sorting out Max here.' Sam removed the paper-clip, examined the glowing tip then put it back again. 'This is pretty high-tech stuff,' he told his patient. Max was looking increasingly worried. 'Hold the thumb steady for me, Kate.'

The glowing tip of the paper-clip burned a hole instantly through the blackened nail. There was a hiss and a small tendril of steam as the hot metal penetrated through to the trapped blood. Max gave a surprised yelp and Kate covered the nail with a gauze pad as the rest of the blood escaped. Within seconds the nail was white instead of black and Max was smiling. He waggled his thumb experimentally and sighed with relief.

'You'll be right now, mate,' Sam told him. He nodded at Kate. 'Strap it with Elastoplast but keep the tip visible.' Sam turned back to their patient as he left. 'Leave the strapping on for a week but move your thumb frequently. See your GP if the tip changes colour or feels odd. You can expect to lose the whole nail before long.' He gave Max a wave. 'Just aim the hammer better next time, eh?'

Kate ushered Max back to the waiting area a few minutes later. Joe was helping another man out of his seat who was holding a blood-soaked towel to his nose.

'She dose I'b allergic to the dab cats,' the man was telling Joe loudly. 'Ad what does she do? Let's the dab thigs sleep od the bed.'

Kate grinned at Joe. The complete nasal blockage gave the man's voice a comic element. She followed them back as far as the whiteboard.

'I wake ub steezig,' the man shouted irately. 'I'b steezig id the shower. I cut byself shavig for steezig.'

Joe paused to write the man's name beside the box for cubicle four. Kate reached up to remove Max's name from beside number one.

'Cart eat breakfast for steezig.' The man followed Joe into the cubicle and Joe smiled at Kate as he pulled the curtain closed. The tirade was still going on. 'Fidally I'b gettig out of the house ad I steeze ad get a dab dosebleed.'

Kate was still smiling as the radio transmitter crackled beside her. She reached for the microphone.

'St Matthew's Emergency Department. Kate Campbell speaking. What can I do for you?'

'We've got a middle-aged woman,' the voice came back. 'Car rear-ended at speed. Whiplash injury. Probable cervical fracture.'

Sam appeared beside Kate. 'What are the symptoms?' he queried.

'Severe neck pain. Weakness in both arms and tingling in the right leg. We're going to try and stabilise her before we get her out of the car. ETA could be ten to fifteen minutes.'

Kate was only half listening to Sam's advice on stabilising the woman's neck. They had two free cubicles now. Julian hadn't added any information on the case he was seeing. Joe's patient's blocked tones were still floating past the curtain.

'I've tried this,' he was complaining. 'It wote work. I've eved tried ad ice pack. Dab thigs beed bleedig for over ad hour.'

Julian appeared beside Sam again. 'Can't see a thing. Could be just scratched. Might explain the difficulty in swallowing.'

'Get a small piece of cotton wool and soak it in barium,' Sam suggested. 'Get her to swallow it. Might catch on the bone and show up on X-ray.'

Julian looked at the paper onto which Sam was jotting notes. 'What's coming in?'

'Cervical fracture, by the sound of it. Whiplash.'

'Done some Gardner-Wells calipers before?'

'Only once. I'll give Neurosurgery a call. ETA's not for ten minutes or so. They've got to get her out of the car, and I've told them to make sure of the splinting before they even try to move her.'

Kate checked the board again. She would need some more staff in the resus. area. Margo went past with a woman, carrying a small child.

'What cubicle, Kate?'

'One's clear,' Kate said. 'Get Louise to check her if she's free. And I'll need you in Resus. in five minutes.'

The radio crackled again and Sam reached for the microphone. 'That'll be them again.'

But it was a new call.

'We've got a white male, approximately early thirties,' the paramedic informed them. 'Found semi-conscious in Regent's Park. Evidence of heavy alcohol consumption.'

'Glasgow coma scale?' Sam queried.

'Was ten,' the paramedic replied. 'Dropping now. He's uncooperative.'

'Any sign of head injuries?'

'No.'

'Vital signs?'

'Pulse fifty, BP ninety over sixty, skin cold and clammy, pinpoint pupils.'

Julian nudged Sam. 'Hasn't OD'd on alcohol, then.'

Sam pushed the button on the microphone again. 'Any evidence of drug ingestion?'

'No needle marks. Denied taking anything but he's not making much sense now.'

'What's your ETA?'

'We're in a traffic snarl right now. Looks like you might be getting some more customers from an accident up the road. We'll be at least ten minutes.'

Joe came out of cubicle four shaking his head. They could all hear his patient, wailing.

'I'b bleedig to death id here! Dab cats!'

'I'm having trouble controlling this nose bleed,' Joe told them. 'Can someone have a look?'

'Suck out the blood,' Sam instructed. 'Soak some gauze in about 4 ml of 4% lignocaine with 1/2 ml of 1/1000 adrenaline. Pack the nose and leave it for five minutes. I'll be in by then. I'm just going to call Neurosurgery.'

'Better give Roger a call as well,' Julian added. 'I suppose you'd like the fracture?'

Kate was already moving towards Resus. She heard Julian's sigh. 'I guess I'll have the OD, then. Another no-hoper to patch up.'

The woman was terrified. 'I'm going to be paralysed, aren't I?'

'It's too soon to know anything,' Kate told her gently. 'There's a lot of swelling going on right now.'

'But I can't move my arms.'

Kate wiped away the tears, streaming down the woman's cheeks. 'I know it's hard but try to stay calm. The most important thing right now is to get your neck as stable as possible and make sure the damage doesn't get any worse.' Kate was watching the patient carefully. She hoped the woman's distress wasn't masking any deterioration in her breathing. 'Do you understand what the doctors are going to do?'

Her patient groaned fearfully. 'It's going to hurt, isn't it? They're going to put screws into my skull.'

'It might be uncomfortable but it won't hurt,' Kate promised. 'Getting the local anaesthetic in will be the worst bit.'

Kate could hear the sounds of Julian's overdose case in the next bed. She'd caught a glimpse of the unshaven and thin male as he'd been transferred to the bed.

'Totally flaccid,' she heard Julian mutter. 'I don't like his breathing much either. Let's give him another dose of Narcan. Hey!' His voice was raised sharply. 'What's your name? What have you taken?'

Sam was scrubbing, in conversation with the neurosurgeon. Margo came over to Kate, carrying a kidney dish. Kate touched an area around her patient's ears. 'Shave it back this far on both sides,' she instructed Margo, 'and then paint it. Sam will be ready to start in a minute.'

Kate saw the police officer come in through the swing doors. She went to intercept him.

'We found these pill containers in a rubbish bin near where that chap was found.' The police officer bypassed Kate and handed the bottles to Joe.

'Pretty heavy duty analgesics here.' Joe read out the labels. 'Morphine sulphate tablets and pethidine. They're hospital-issued. Welsh authority.'

'I need some help here,' Julian shouted. He picked up an ambu bag and mask and replaced his patient's oxygen mask. 'We've got a respiratory arrest. Endotracheal tube, size eight.'

Kate dived for the tube. She started ripping open the packaging as Julian reached for a laryngoscope.

'Name on the label's Peter Ryder.' Joe dropped the containers on the end of the bed. 'May have been stolen or sold, of course.'

Joe's voice faded as Kate heard a roaring sound in her ears. It couldn't be. She stared at the face on the pillow, now visible as Julian reached behind her. The lack of hair and the growth of stubble was wrong and the face was too thin, but the identity of the man was instantly—and horribly—clear. Peter!

Kate took a step backwards instinctively. She knocked into Julian's arm and the laryngoscope crashed to the floor.

'For God's sake, Kate!' Julian's shout was outraged.

Joe pulled back the side-curtain and hurriedly picked up another laryngoscope.

'Give me the tube,' Julian snapped.

But Kate was frozen. She barely heard the consultant. Her eyes were still riveted on the face before her, a face now turning blue through lack of oxygen. She felt the package she was holding being torn from her hands and knew she had moved because the trolley beside her had tipped over. The crash of instruments and broken glass only added to the confusion.

'Get her out of here,' Julian barked. '*Now!*'

She could see Sam. Gloved and gowned. Pausing as he held aloft a syringe of lignocaine. He was staring at her, his expression horrified. Kate felt herself bumped as more staff moved in to respond to Julian's terse orders. She felt hands on her own arms as she was pulled clear of the scene. It wasn't until she was through the swing doors of the resus. area that she realised it had been the police officer who had responded to Julian's request for her removal. Louise Grant was on the other side of the doors.

'What's going on? Are you all right, Kate?'

Kate nodded dumbly. She could still hear the sounds of the chaos she had left behind her. Louise could hear it as well. After another worried glance at Kate she moved swiftly into Resus.

The police officer finally let go of Kate's arms.

'You'd better sit down for a bit,' he suggested awkwardly. He watched as she slowly sank onto a chair beside the central desk and buried her face in her hands. 'Can I get you a drink of water or something?'

Kate shook her head. Her horrified reaction was fading, only to be replaced with the realisation of how appalling her behaviour had been. If she'd been in some way prepared it wouldn't have happened. It shouldn't have happened in any case. Her emotional shell had already been cracked, thanks to Sam. Now the past had caught up with her and shattered her professional defences.

She was always the one who took the most harrowing cases, the most severe emergencies, helped the most distressed relatives. Kate could always cope. Totally competent, completely dependable. How could she possibly explain this? She didn't want to try and explain it. What was the point, anyway? It was totally inexcusable.

'Excuse me?'

Kate looked up slowly. The police officer had gone. A young man she didn't recognise stood beside her.

'I'm John Fraser. ENT registrar. I had a call about an unresponsive epistaxis.' He peered at Kate through his spectacles. 'Nosebleed?' he translated unnecessarily.

'Cubicle four,' Kate said wearily. She wondered how many people had gone by, unnoticed, as she'd sat at the desk. If they weren't all discussing her behaviour already they would be soon enough. Kate stood up and made her way to the common room. She wasn't going to be of any use to the patients right now and she had no intention of compounding the situation she was already in. How many times had she sent juniors in here, even during frantically busy periods, for some time out when things had become too much for them? It had never occurred to her that she might ever need it herself.

She was alone in the common room. She was still alone thirty minutes later when Julian Calder burst through the door. He was followed closely by Sam.

'You can go home,' Julian informed Kate. 'Collect your things and go.'

'You can't do this!' Sam seemed to be repeating something he had already said many times.

'I most certainly can. I'm quite within my rights to suspend any member of staff from duties if they're incompetent or a danger to patients. Nurse Campbell here has demonstrated both attributes.'

Sam gave a disgusted snort. 'You know that's rubbish as well as I do.'

'The evidence speaks for itself. Not only did she not assist with a respiratory arrest, she created a situation that was life-threatening for Mr Ryder. She—'

'Rot!' Sam interjected. 'It was a—'

Julian cut him off. 'Not only did she create a life-threatening situation for Mr Ryder, you know perfectly well that she added to the distress your own patient was experiencing. If you hadn't been able to prevent her moving her head to try and see what was going on the results could have been catastrophic.'

Kate closed her eyes. She could imagine only too well the effect her behaviour must have had on everybody in the resus. area. It was quite true. She could have been responsible for turning Sam's patient into a quadriplegic.

Julian was still shouting. 'There's no room for

nursing staff in an emergency situation who can't even respond to a direct request for a piece of standard equipment.'

'There's got to be a reason.' Sam was also as close to shouting as Kate had ever heard him. 'For God's sake, man! Kate's well-being should be of more concern to you right now than trying to punish her for a totally out of character mess-up.'

'There's absolutely no excuse for that sort of incompetence.'

Sam ignored Julian. He dropped to a squat in front of Kate's chair. 'Are you all right, Katy? Did you feel sick or faint? Have you got any visual disturbances?'

Kate shook her head. She couldn't look at Sam.

'Did you recognise him? Peter Ryder? Do you know him?'

Kate shook her head more firmly.

Julian made an exasperated sound. 'You're suspended from duties, Kate. And I'll be doing my best to make it permanent. I'm going to get Jeff Merrick out of his meeting immediately and inform him of the action I've taken. I know it's precisely what he would have done himself.'

Sam straightened. He towered over Kate. 'I'm not going to let you do this, Julian.'

'It's got nothing to do with you, old chap.' Julian pulled the door open. 'You're not even officially part of this department. Simply a guest. It's none of your business so keep your nose out of it.'

'No way!' Sam didn't even look at Kate as he followed Julian out the door. 'I'm making it my business. And what's more—'

The voices faded as the door shut.

Kate took a long shaky breath in and then got to her feet.

It felt odd, changing to go home in the middle of the morning. It was even stranger to walk through a department where no one would even catch her eye. The atmosphere was almost hushed. The storm had finally broken and everyone had run for cover.

Sam caught up with Kate as she slipped out through the ambulance bay doors. He caught her arm.

'Kate, wait! Jeff Merrick is as appalled as I am at what Julian's done.'

Kate swallowed. 'What did he say?'

'He wants to see you.' Sam looked uncomfortable. 'But not just yet. He thinks that a day or two away might be a good idea to let Julian calm down and for him to find out exactly what happened.' Sam squeezed the arm he was still holding. 'I'm not going to let him get away with this, Kate. What exactly did happen?'

'I failed to cope in an emergency situation.'

'Yes—but *why*?'

Kate pulled her arm free. 'I don't know.'

'Yes, you do,' Sam said angrily. Then he sighed heavily. 'If you don't want to trust me enough to tell me then I can't force you. If you don't want to fight your own battles I can't force you to do that either.' His face tightened. 'Right now I'm angry enough to poke my nose in and fight this one for you. Because I'm fed up with the way people behave in this place. And because I care about you, Kate. More than you care about yourself, I think.' Sam stepped away from Kate. 'And when I've sorted it out you can expect to hear from me. Because then, Kate Campbell, you and I are going to talk. And I mean *really* talk.'

*   *   *

The side-room in the oncology ward was unusually stark.

There was no one visiting. There were no flowers, no cards—nothing to relieve the clinical appearance of the small room. The bed was unruffled, the linen smoothed over the shape of the unmoving figure. An IV line snaked under the covers. The heavily shadowed eyes were closed in the emaciated face.

'Peter?'

The eyes opened slowly. The dull expression remained unchanged as Peter Ryder regarded his visitor.

'I'm Sam. I was in the emergency department when you came in this morning.'

'So?'

'So I wanted to see how you were.'

'Well, you've seen. Don't expect me to thank you. I didn't want to be resuscitated. I'll just have to try again now.'

'Your doctor tells me they think they can adjust your medication so that the pain and nausea will be better controlled. You may find you're glad of a bit of extra time.'

Peter's expression suggested otherwise.

'We had a bit of a problem, sorting you out, in actual fact,' Sam said casually. 'You had quite an effect on one of our nurses.'

Peter's snort was disbelieving. Then his lips twitched. 'Well, I've had my share, I suppose, but she must have been a bit desperate to fancy me in this state.'

'That's not quite what I meant. I think this nurse wasn't very happy to see you. She was distressed enough not to be able to do her job. Now she's been suspended from duties because of it.'

'What's that got to do with me?'

'Her name is Kate. Kate Campbell.' Sam didn't miss the flicker in Peter's expression. 'Mean anything to you?'

'Nah!'

'But you know her?'

'Look, I'm tired.' Peter closed his eyes. 'Do me a favour and get lost.'

'I'm not going anywhere,' Sam said evenly. He sat on the chair beside the bed to emphasise his point. 'Listen, mate. Kate's in a spot of trouble and I think it's got something to do with you.'

'Kate Campbell makes her own trouble.'

'I thought you said you didn't know her.'

'Nah. I said she didn't mean anything to me.'

'But she did once?'

Peter's eyes opened again slowly. 'Could have. She blew it.'

'How?'

'Dumped me. Silly bitch. I had the ring and everything.'

'Engagement ring?'

'You said it.' Peter sighed in disgust. 'What's the point of this? It's ancient history. I'm out of it—or soon will be.'

'You're happy to leave unfinished business?'

'It was finished a long time ago.'

'Not for Kate.' Sam was angry but he kept his voice under firm control. He knew he had touched on the key to her secret, and his sympathy for Kate outweighed the regret he felt for the man before him with terminal cancer.

'Course it is. She was the one who finished it. Wouldn't even talk to me. Even her mother thought she was mad. Told me so herself.'

'Why did she think Kate was mad?'

'For dumping me.'

'Why did she do that?'

'Ask her.'

'I'm asking you.'

'I dunno.' Peter's face twisted with sudden anger. 'I never knew. It wasn't as if I'd got her pregnant.'

'But you could have?'

'Not bloody likely. First time it was—and last!'

'Not good, then, eh?'

The smirk grated on Sam. 'I thought it was. Bit rough's fine by me—know what I mean? Not that I remember that much. I'd had a few, you know? Dutch courage.'

'Yeah, I know.' Sam tried to sound sympathetic. 'Kate didn't like it, then?'

'Stupid bitch. Had the nerve to tell me I'd raped her.' Peter snorted incredulously. 'As if! I mean, we'd been going out for years. You can't rape someone you're planning to marry.'

'Is that right?' Sam was holding his temper with difficulty. 'Was it what she wanted at the time?'

Peter shrugged. 'I dunno. I don't really care any more. What does it matter?'

Sam leaned over Peter. His voice was low, his contempt clear. 'It matters, mate, because you stuffed up someone else's life. You may not remember what happened but I think you were more than a "bit rough". I think you hurt Kate Campbell very badly. You hurt her physically, but what really makes me spit is the effect you've had on her life emotionally.

I think her experience with you was enough to convince her she could never have a relationship with anyone else.' Sam stood abruptly. 'I think you're a prize bastard, Mr Ryder. You might be ''out of it'' soon but you gave Kate a life sentence.'

Peter Ryder was gaping at Sam's vehemence. 'What's it to you, anyway?'

'I happen to think she's served enough of her sentence. She deserves to get more out of life than what she's had so far. Nobody deserves to be haunted by a bastard like you.'

'You can't talk to me like that. I'm going to make a complaint.'

'You do that, mate. But I'm not actually part of the department here officially. I'm simply a guest.' Sam paused at the door. 'Maybe a short time is all I need to do someone a good turn. To give someone something good to remember. Think about it, Peter.' Sam opened the door. 'Maybe a short time is all you need as well.'

CHAPTER SEVEN

'I KNOW all about it, Kate.'

'About what?'

'About what happened between you and Peter Ryder.'

Kate's eyes dropped to the off-licence carrier bag Sam was cradling. She could feel the colour creeping up her cheeks.

'Are you going to ask me in?'

Kate stepped away from the door. Sam moved past her decisively. 'God, it's cold in here.' He turned and looked at Kate sternly. 'Have you just been sitting around, being cold and miserable all day?'

'I've been out walking,' Kate said quietly. 'I had a lot to think about.'

'You get that fire going, then.' Sam disappeared into the kitchen. 'I'm going to find some glasses.'

Kate was sitting on the floor in front of the gas fire when Sam returned. She accepted the glass of wine with a nod of thanks and watched as Sam sat beside her. For such a large man he moved with astonishing grace. She had the impression that he was entirely comfortable with himself and totally confident in what he was doing. She took a sip of the wine, waiting for Sam to break the silence. But he simply sat, the glow of the fire reflecting in his glass each time he raised it.

Finally Kate broke the silence. 'Busy day?' she enquired.

'The usual.' Sam glanced sideways. 'Interesting atmosphere.'

'I'll bet.' Kate could imagine only too well the gossip that would be circulating. How much did they all know?

'Not a popular man, our Julian,' Sam said casually. 'You've got a lot of friends there, Kate, even if you have tried to keep them all away. There's a great deal of respect for you as well.'

'There won't be,' Kate muttered darkly. 'When they find out they'll just feel sorry for me.'

'Why should they do that?'

'Because I fell apart over something that happened ten years ago. Something that most people would be able to get over.'

'Rape isn't something that most people get over, Katy.'

The glass shook in Kate's hand. Hurriedly she raised it to her lips and took a gulp. 'How did you find out?'

'I had a little chat with Peter.'

'He admitted he raped me?' Kate's tone was incredulous. 'When I accused him at the time he just laughed.'

'The bloke's a jerk,' Sam said calmly. 'He thinks rape is something that can only happen between strangers. He does admit to being too drunk to remember exactly what happened.'

'So what makes you assume it was rape?' Kate stared into the fire.

'I think I know you quite well now, Katy. The way you react to people—your lifestyle—pointed to someone with something they wanted to hide. I also knew there had to be a reason why you were so de-

termined that our relationship didn't get physical.'
Sam grinned and winked. 'When it was so obvious
you fancied me as much as I did you.' He sobered
again. 'Then I saw the fear in your face when you
recognised Peter. It was pretty easy to fill in the gaps
when I went and paid him a visit.'

'I suppose everybody knows, then?'

Sam reached over to refill Kate's wine glass. 'Only
me. And I don't know everything so why don't you
share your secret and fill me in? How did you get
hooked up with such a creep in the first place?'

'He wasn't a creep,' Kate said slowly. 'I'd known
him most of my life. His father was the senior partner
in my father's law firm. Our mothers were close
friends. We saw a lot of each other. We were
friends.'

'So when did that change?'

'Not until he went away to university. We only
saw each other in the holidays. My parents started
letting me go out at night then. They'd always been
very strict about that. But Peter was trustworthy.
They all assumed we would end up getting married.'

'Did you assume that as well?'

'I suppose I did.' Kate sighed heavily. 'It was all
very comfortable—safe. Everybody liked Peter and
he was all set to join the law firm when he got his
degree. He had a good future, as my mother was so
fond of telling me.'

'Did you go out with anybody else?'

'No. Just Peter. We were going steady by the time
I was seventeen. It all seemed to be going well. We
were still friends but that changed gradually. Nothing
too heavy, but I knew we would sleep together some
time. I wanted to…' Kate bit her lip. 'He didn't tell

me his parents were out of town that night. We'd been out to dinner. When we got to his place it all seemed set up. It made me nervous. Peter had been drinking. I hadn't because I was driving. It all got out of hand.' Kate was hugging her knees, her glass forgotten.

'You told him you didn't want to?' Sam prompted gently.

Kate nodded miserably. A tear escaped and rolled down the side of her nose. 'I begged him to stop,' she whispered. 'I was crying. It only seemed to make him more excited. I was still crying when he'd finished. He told me that I was a prude. That...that I was frigid.'

'And you believed him?' Sam sounded outraged.

'I was confused and frightened,' Kate said brokenly. 'And everybody seemed to be on his side. In the end I decided that it must have been my fault—that there was something wrong with me.'

'Did you go to the police?'

'God, no! How could I? His parents were my parents' best friends. They all thought the sun shone out of Peter. My mother thought I was trying to find an excuse to explain a pregnancy. Reputations had to be protected. Especially theirs,' she added bitterly.

'Didn't you have anyone you could talk to?'

Kate shook her head, the tears rolling faster. 'Even my best friend, Elizabeth, didn't believe me. She said the first time hadn't been that great for her either but that it got better, and I'd probably only made it worse by being so uptight. And she said I must have known what was expected when I went home with him. She thought there was something wrong with me, too.

When I wouldn't talk to Peter she started going out with him herself.'

'More fool her,' Sam commented.

Kate's shoulders shook as she broke into sobs. She felt the heaviness of Sam's arms around her and allowed herself to be drawn closer. There was nothing left to hide. Sam stroked her head as he held her.

'Did nobody ever show you that it wasn't supposed to be like that, Katy? Could you never trust anyone enough to let them close again?'

'I tried once—a few years later.' Kate's voice was muffled against Sam's shoulder. 'His name was James. I thought I could do it but I got scared. He thought I was teasing him and got angry.'

Sam held her tighter. 'And since then?'

Kate shook her head. 'I've never tried. Never wanted to until…until I met you.'

Sam kissed her forehead but Kate sat up and moved back. 'It's no good, Sam. Surely you can understand that now?'

'Nope.' Sam picked up his glass and raised it in a salute to Kate. 'You've trusted me enough to tell me your story, Katy, so trust me a little bit more. Everything's going to be all right.'

Kate smiled shakily. 'I wish I could believe you.'

'You will.' Sam sounded confident. 'Have you had anything to eat today?'

'No.'

'Let's go and find a take-away, then.'

'OK, in a minute.' Kate picked up her glass again and then eyed Sam. 'How did you really know, Sam?'

'About Peter?'

'Not just that—other things. You see things other

people can't. It was the first thing I noticed about you. That first day when you appeared in Emergency and you made that comment about Julian? It was quite scary that you could have noticed something like that so easily. I felt threatened.' Kate smiled shyly. 'And then I started to like it. It was like some invisible communication that was always there.'

Sam shrugged lightly. 'It comes from being able to listen, I suppose. Most people are too busy talking themselves to try it. You've got it too, you know. That's why you noticed it in me. We're two of a kind. Joe's got it as well for his own reasons.'

'What are my reasons?' Kate was curious.

'You cut yourself off from people. It left you in your own little corner, watching and listening to the rest of the world instead of taking part.'

'You make me sound like a recluse,' Kate protested. 'I might live alone but I'm not entirely anti-social.'

'Yes, you are—emotionally. I'm not blaming you. I think you coped the best way you could with a disaster that no one helped you with.'

'So what's your excuse, then?'

Sam grinned broadly. 'I grew up with five women who never stopped talking. I couldn't get a word in edgeways so I just learned to watch and listen in-stead. Guess it got to be a habit.'

'You talk enough now!'

'Too much sometimes,' Sam agreed. 'Doesn't mean I don't notice things. Now, are we going to eat or am I going to die of starvation?' Sam held out his hand and helped Kate to her feet. He kept hold of her hand. 'Are we friends again, Katy?'

'Are you sure you want to be?'

Sam nodded. His look was serious. 'Do you trust me?'

It was Kate's turn to nod. With the gesture came the realisation that she did, indeed, mean it. And with that knowledge came a bubble of hope for what the future might hold.

'Sit down, Kate.'

The summons had been only twenty-four hours in coming and Kate hadn't been particularly reassured by the thumbs-up signal Sam had given her as she'd tried to slip through the department unnoticed. It had only been a few days since she'd been in this office with Joe, but it had not been her performance under scrutiny then. And she hadn't been alone. She relaxed only slightly when the emergency department director smiled at her.

'You've caused a bit of a stir, Nurse Campbell.'

Kate swallowed hard. 'I know. I'm sorry. My behaviour was inexcusable.'

'Oh, I wouldn't say that.' Jeff Merrick leaned back in his chair. 'Unfortunate, yes, but hardly inexcusable. And I want to thank you.'

'Sorry?' Kate thought she'd misheard.

'I've spoken to quite a few people since yesterday. I've learned more about this department in twenty-four hours than I have in the last twenty-four months.'

'It's an excellent department,' Kate said quickly. 'One that I've been proud to work in.'

'And will continue to do so, I hope.' Jeff smiled wryly. 'I have no intention of considering Dr Calder's demands that your suspension becomes permanent.'

Kate was silent. She suddenly wondered whether she even wanted to work with Julian any more. Maybe she'd had enough and, like Sam, was fed up with the behaviour of the junior consultant. Sharing her secret had removed part of an obstacle she'd considered insurmountable. She'd waited ten years for someone to tell her that it hadn't been her fault and that everything would be all right. She wasn't sure *how* things could be made right but Sam's confidence was contagious. Maybe this was her chance to break the mould and change her life for the better.

'You may be interested to know that the demands for your reinstatement have been just as vigorous—and not just by our antipodean visitor.' Jeff's smile was now amused. Sam might just as well have been in the room—the comment evoked an almost tangible presence.

Kate found herself returning the smile. 'He's a good friend,' she offered, by way of an explanation.

'He's not your only friend, Kate. You'd be surprised at the level of support from other staff members. I was surprised myself.' Jeff leaned forward and rested his elbows on his desk. 'Not by the glowing reports of your competence and abilities. I've known that all along. What surprised me was the situation with regard to Julian's treatment of you.' He drummed his fingers on his desk. 'And not only you. I've had several nurses come forward and make complaints about what could only be considered direct sexual harassment.'

Kate nodded slowly. 'I should have said something last week, I suppose, but it was never blatant. It didn't interfere with the running of the department, and the other girls didn't seem bothered. It's very difficult when it's a consultant involved. I thought I might just seem…I don't know, a spoilsport or something.'

Jeff nodded. 'His suspension of you was the final straw for Margo, at any rate. She had quite a lot to tell me. And the student—Bonnie, is it? She was upset enough by Julian's approaches to consult her supervisor, who then came to me.' Jeff sighed heavily. 'Anyway, the matter has been dealt with. Julian is aware that the matter may go before the medical disciplinary association should there be any further complaints, and he has agreed to a move away from the emergency department.'

Kate's mouth dropped open slightly.

'There's a locum on Anaesthetics he's agreed to fill in the meantime. Sam has kindly offered to act as Locum in emergency until we can find a permanent replacement, so things should run a little more smoothly now. Or, at least, they will when you're back on duty. Can you start immediately?'

Kate nodded eagerly. 'I'll go and get changed.'

'Good.' Jeff stood at the same time as Kate. 'I would have overriden Julian's actions, no matter what anyone else had said,' he told Kate. 'I value you as a staff member very highly. I would hate to lose you—especially now that we've finally had the nod to set up our flying squad.'

'Thank you.' Kate felt embarrassed but then straightened her shoulders. 'I'm not planning on going anywhere.'

'We'll see,' Jeff said enigmatically. Then his tone became curious. 'There was one other person who seemed keen to see this situation resolved.'

'Oh?'

'The patient, Peter Ryder. He asked to see me early this morning and the ward staff contacted me. I must say I was intrigued. He seemed to know you.'

'What did he say?' Kate queried nervously.

'He said that he was to blame, not you, and he wanted the matter dropped.' Jeff's gaze was puzzled. 'I asked him how he knew there was any problem and it seems that our friend Sam was involved.'

'Mmm.' Kate glanced away. 'He seems to like getting involved.'

'That certainly seems to be the case, as far as you're concerned.' Jeff shook his head but then smiled. 'I can't say I understand what's going on but I'm not going to enquire any further. I've been around long enough to know when I can trust someone, I hope, and Dr Marshall is about as high on the list as you are.' He put a hand on Kate's shoulder as he ushered her out the door. 'And that's pretty high.'

Kate eyed the busy department below them. She was impatient to get back into uniform but paused to smile at her boss. 'He's pretty high on my list too,' she confided.

Joe was the first person to greet Kate when she emerged somewhat tentatively from the locker room. Nobody had spoken to her, or even looked at her, when she'd crept away in disgrace the day before. Despite Jeff Merrick's report of the support she'd been shown, Kate thought her reception might prove difficult. She felt that she'd been knocked off her perch, exposed as being more human than she had ever allowed them to see before. She had deliberately avoided friendship with these people. Would their professional relationship have survived the events of the last day?

Joe's usually reserved smile was replaced by a broad grin when he spotted Kate. He put down the tray of blood samples he was carrying and enfolded her in an enthusiastic hug. 'Thank goodness,' he said. 'You're back.'

To Kate's astonishment, Margo rushed over and also hugged her. Then Jude. And Louise. Even Patsy left her post at Reception—an unheard of neglect of duty—and gave Kate a very hard squeeze.

'About time this place was sorted out,' she said gruffly. 'Welcome back, Kate.'

The welcome and the affection were overwhelming. Kate was blinking back tears as the staff quickly dispersed to continue their pressing duties. Then Sam appeared from a cubicle. She smiled and shook her head, bemused.

'I had no idea they felt like that,' she said quietly.

'You've never given them a chance to show it,' Sam told her. 'Sometimes it takes a crisis to break down barriers.' He jerked his head towards the cubicle he'd just left. 'Now, come with me, please, Nurse. I've got a lovely laceration in here that could do with an expert seamstress.'

Kate was soon drawn back into a typically busy shift. She delighted in the work and the occasional interruption only added to the special feel of the day. Margo caught her as she was collecting a tray of dressings to deal with a minor burn.

'We're going to the pub after work to celebrate.'

'Is it someone's birthday?'

Margo grinned. 'It feels like it. We're celebrating the sorting-out. Julian going—you coming back. Will you come?' A hint of doubt clouded Margo's face. Kate had never joined a purely social staff gathering.

'I'd love to,' Kate responded. And she meant it.

Sam caught her as she was updating the information on the whiteboard. 'I just checked on my lady from yesterday with the cervical fracture. The swelling's under control and she's got some movement back in her arms. She'll probably need surgery for complete stabilisation but the odds are that she'll make a very good recovery.'

Kate's smile was very relieved. Thank goodness her actions hadn't made things any worse for Sam's patient. 'That's great news,' she told Sam enthusiastically.

'I thought you'd be pleased.' Sam grinned. In full view of several staff members he put his arm around her waist and planted a kiss on her cheek. Kate was horrified.

'You can't do that here!'

'I just did. Want to see it again?'

'No!' Kate sidestepped Sam's grasp but she was smiling. She looked up in time to see Jude's look of amazement change to one of knowing delight. Sam saw it too.

'It's just impossible to keep a secret in this place,' he said cheerfully.

Kate watched Jude duck into the common room. 'Only if you don't want to,' she muttered. 'It'll be all over the place in two minutes.'

'Secrets are like sweeping dirt under the rug,' Sam said sternly. 'Sooner or later you have to sort out the lump.'

'Look who's talking!'

'What do you mean?' Sam's eyes were roundly innocent.

'What do the S and A stand for, Dr Marshall?'

'Ah!' Sam tapped the side of his nose. 'Some secrets are in one's best interests not to know.'

'Your philosophy has as many holes in it as sieve.' Kate shook her head in amusement and reached for the phone. 'I wonder if they've got a bed ready for us in Orthopaedics yet.'

'Just ask Tommy Bragan,' Sam advised.

Kate's finger was poised over the telephone buttons. 'Who's Tommy Bragan?'

Sam's grin was more muppet-like than usual. 'He was in my kindergarten class. He was the last person who found out what my initials stood for.'

Kate's gaze was centred on Sam's back as he headed away from her. 'So, what happened to Tommy Bragan?'

Sam's head shook sadly. 'Took a long time for his nose to stop bleeding.'

The last interruption Kate had was from Jeff. It was less pleasant than the earlier interchanges. They were alone in the resus. area as Kate finished clearing up.

'I had another call from the oncology ward,' he told Kate, 'concerning Peter Ryder. He's being transferred to a hospital in Wales this evening. He's asked to see you before he goes.'

Kate shook her head quickly. 'I don't want to see him.'

Jeff nodded. 'That's fine. You don't have to.'

'Why is he in Oncology?' Kate queried. 'I thought he was an overdose case.'

'He was. He was simply trying to hasten the inevitable. Peter Ryder's dying, Kate. He has osteosarcoma. Rather a nasty way to go, bone cancer.

Very painful. Incurable. I doubt that he has more than a month or two at the most.'

Sam stopped at the entrance to the ward. 'Are you sure you don't want me to come in with you?'

'I won't be long,' Kate said quietly. 'It'll help just to know you're here, waiting.'

'I'll be here,' Sam promised, 'but I'd rather be with you.'

'It's something I should face on my own.' Kate tried to sound confident. 'It's the last chance I'll get.'

'Just don't expect too much,' Sam warned. 'You know the truth and so do I. It doesn't matter what he thinks.'

But it did matter. Kate stopped at the open door to Peter's room and stared at the figure on the bed. He'd blamed her for what had happened. Everyone had blamed her. She'd ended up blaming herself. For the first time Kate felt she could justify redirecting the blame. The anger she now felt was the accumulation of years of suppression.

'You asked to see me.' The voice was so cold Kate didn't recognise it as her own.

'They told me you weren't coming.' Peter sounded tired.

'I wasn't going to. I never wanted to see you again.'

'You made that clear ten years ago. What changed your mind?'

'A friend thought I should. He thought it might help me to…to…' Kate's voice wobbled. She wasn't sure if it was due to anger or distress. She took a step into the room as she tried to control herself.

'Was I that much of a bastard, Kate?'

'Yes.' Kate's voice was firm again. 'Yes, you were.'

Peter closed his eyes. He sighed heavily, before opening them again. 'Have you hated me all these years?'

'Yes. But not just because of what you did to me. I hated you because you destroyed my trust in all the people that mattered. I hated you because you made me hate myself. That's something I can't forgive.'

'So why did you come to see me?'

'I wanted to make sure you understood,' Kate said more quietly. 'I suppose I wanted you to take some of the blame—something that you never did at the time.'

Peter's face twisted in pain. Kate assumed it was physical. She was reminded of the terminal state of this young man's disease and an unwelcome sense of pity crowded in on her other emotions.

'I hadn't even thought about it for years,' Peter said finally. 'Not until that chap came to see me yesterday. Unfinished business, he called it. I had a lot of time to think last night.' Peter closed his eyes again and took several deep breaths, as though gathering strength. 'I had no idea what effect it all had on you. I didn't even remember that much about it. I'm sorry, Kate. I knew it shouldn't have happened that way and I felt guilty about it at the time. It was just easier to get angry and blame you. And then you left and there wasn't anything I could do anyway. I'm sorry, Kate,' he repeated.

'It's a bit late for an apology,' Kate said bitterly, 'but I guess that was what I came for.'

'It's a bit late for everything for me,' Peter said wearily. 'I suppose you think this is all I deserve.'

'Nobody deserves this,' Kate responded. 'I'm sorry for you, Peter.'

'I missed you after you left.' Peter spoke with his eyes shut. His voice was sleepy. 'Nothing went quite right after that. I dropped out of law school. Did you know I married Elizabeth?'

'I saw you together at my father's funeral.' That memory was a bitter one, which she'd carried for years as well. Her ex-best friend had been heavily pregnant. She'd gone a lot further than merely defending Peter against Kate's accusations.

'You weren't there.' Peter's eyes flickered open briefly. 'Your mother never forgave you for that.'

'I was there,' Kate told him. 'I sat at the back of the church and I left straight after the service.'

'Why didn't you speak to your mother?'

'I couldn't forgive her—for taking your side instead of mine. I haven't seen her since.'

Peter was staring at her. 'I had no idea.' He shook his head very slowly. 'She misses you.'

'How would you know?'

'I saw her a couple of weeks ago. I got sick of my own mother, fussing and crying around me. That's why I decided to get away and get it over with. On my own. But I'm going home again.' He looked away. 'Don't die on your own, Kate. I wouldn't recommend it.'

'Where's Elizabeth?'

'She left me—years ago. I haven't seen the kids since. Maybe I'll have a go at sorting that one out as well.'

Kate sighed. Peter was clearly exhausted and in pain. His breathing was rapid, his voice becoming strained.

'I'd better go,' she said softly. 'I've got someone waiting for me.'

'Don't hate me, Kate.' The words were slurred now.

'I don't think I do,' Kate told him. 'Not any more.'

There was no response. Kate stood for a moment. It was true. The hate she'd felt had gone. The anger had also faded. She was left with the pity she felt for the wasted life before her. But she was also left with a sense of resolution, a peace with herself that no one else could have given her.

'Goodbye, Peter,' she whispered. 'And thank you.'

CHAPTER EIGHT

'YOU never told me you had a car! How many more secrets do you have?'

Sam's tone was accusatory but Kate just shrugged. 'It wasn't a secret. You never asked. I don't use it in London. It's not worth the hassle when the public transport's so good. I've thought of getting rid of it quite often.'

'Why didn't you, then?'

'It's great to be able to get out of town for a day or two like this and, besides, I've had it for ten years—since it was new.'

'You got a brand-new car when you were eighteen? How did you manage that?'

'It was a birthday present.' Kate smiled. 'More of a bribe, really. If I got to be eighteen, without drinking, smoking or losing my virginity, it was to be my prize.'

'You had to be a virgin as well?' Sam's eyebrows disappeared under his mop of hair.

'It wasn't exactly in the contract,' Kate admitted, 'but it was certainly implied. My mother was very concerned about reputations. Especially theirs. Keep an eye on the signs, Sam. We need to turn off the M4 soon and get onto the A419.' She glanced sideways at her passenger. 'Are you sure you're not getting cramp?'

'Sure am,' Sam groaned. 'Mini Clubmans were never made to carry people my size.'

'It's been a great car,' Kate countered. 'It's taken me thousands of miles and never broken down.'

Sam eyed the traffic on the busy motorway. The Mini's tiny wipers were working fast to keep the windscreen clear of the light drizzle. 'Ever had an accident? Some of these drivers are terrible!'

'Never,' Kate announced proudly. 'I carry a good emergency kit in case I see someone else's, but I've never even used that.'

'What do you carry?'

'Usual dressings, a cervical collar, couple of airways, some haemacell and giving sets, bag and mask, cannulas, syringes, tourniquets and a limited range of drugs.'

Sam whistled. 'I'm impressed.'

'I did a course last year,' Kate explained, 'when Jeff first tried to set up a flying squad. I updated everything then and got clearance for carrying things like narcotics.'

Sam twisted with some difficulty and peered into the tiny back seat. 'I'm even more impressed with where you put it.'

Kate laughed. 'It takes up the whole boot. That's why all our stuff is on the back seat.' She glanced at Sam as he turned back and tried to adjust his position, with little success.

'We'll stop soon and give you a chance to stretch your legs.'

'We could have taken a train, you know.'

'I might need to escape in a hurry.' Kate wasn't smiling. 'I didn't want to be dependent on a time-table.'

'Fair enough. Though you'll have me for back-up.' He rested a large hand gently on Kate's knee. 'I'm proud of you, Katy. Going to see your mother after all these years takes a lot of courage.'

'It's Peter's doing,' Kate reminded him. 'If he hadn't seen Mother and explained everything she wouldn't have written. She didn't even have any idea where I was.'

'She's obviously missed you.' Sam had read the letter almost as often as Kate during the week she'd carried it around with her, pondering her response.

The letter had arrived two weeks after Peter Ryder had been transferred back to Wales. Two weeks in which the team atmosphere of the emergency department had continued to flourish. Kate was thoroughly enjoying the new rapport she had with her colleagues. Even more, she was enjoying the new phase of her relationship with Sam. Their friendship was openly acknowledged, their physical contact frequent but comfortably casual. Hand-holding was automatic, kisses gentle and controlled.

'I won't do anything you don't want me to, Kate,' Sam had promised. 'One of these days, when you trust me enough, you'll be ready for more.'

'I do trust you,' Kate had protested. 'You're the best friend I've ever had. I've never told anybody the things I've told you.'

'There's still a barrier that only you can cross,' Sam had said quietly, 'and I'm not going to push you over it. Just remember that.'

Kate treasured the promise and allowed herself to enjoy his company wholeheartedly. It wasn't difficult. The only shadow was time. Sam's visit was more than half over and in a matter of weeks he was due to return to the other side of the world. Time was against her but Kate refused to dwell on it. She would make the most of what she was offered. She was too happy to consider any alternative. When Sam had suggested he accompany her on this visit to see her mother Kate hadn't attempted to persuade him otherwise, even though she knew how uncomfortable he would be in her tiny car.

The traffic across the four lanes was heavy but for the most part was travelling steadily and reasonably slowly due to the wet conditions. Some juggling was going on in the two faster lanes and Sam shook his head at the impatience of some drivers who stayed in the fast lane, flashing their headlights to order slower vehicles to move left. Kate was in the left lane as usual. The Clubman was no speedster normally and was carrying a lot of extra weight with her large passenger.

A lorry up ahead was moving even more slowly, however, and Kate cast an eye around the next lane to make sure there would be space to pass it. A blue hatchback was a little ahead of her in the second lane and a bright green minibus was nearly level with the Clubman. Kate would have to wait for it to get past her. The flashing headlights of a black vehicle in the extreme right-hand lane caught her eye and she watched the driver's behaviour for a few seconds.

A white sedan was unresponsive to the demand and the sleek, black vehicle Kate was observing moved into the next lane and shot past it on the left. It swerved back into the fast lane and then began to flash its lights again at a van which was now providing a new obstacle to its desired speed.

'I don't believe it,' Kate muttered. The brake lights of the offending black car glowed as it was forced to slow. Clearly irritated at the new delay, the driver of the black car then moved left to repeat the earlier manoeuvre. This time, however, he misjudged the gap in the next lane and Kate and Sam watched in horror as the black car clipped the front of the vehicle it was cutting in front of. The driver of the black sports car lost control instantly and the car skidded and then rolled over the two lanes to its left. The whole incident took only a few seconds and there was too much happening at once for Kate and Sam to register the scale of the disaster.

The lorry swerved away from the rolling car and went onto the grass verge. The white sedan, which had been the victim of the first pass, braked hard in reaction to the unfolding disaster, swerved towards the central reservation of the motorway and was rear-ended at speed by a silver station wagon. The blue hatchback in front of Kate in the second lane also braked sharply, went into a skid and off the road into the back of the lorry.

A motorbike in the third lane, behind the vehicle which had been clipped initially, lost control and crossed into the path of the green minibus. As the minibus swerved, Kate was forced to brake harder and pull to the left. The tiny car bounced onto the grass verge, tipped dangerously as it hit a deep rut and then came to rest against a fence post with a bone-jarring thud. Kate was still gripping the steering-wheel, her knuckles white. The first thing she was aware of was a pain in her upper arm. It was caused by the strength of Sam's grip.

'Are you all right, Kate? Are you hurt?'

'I think I'm fine,' Kate responded quickly. 'What about you?' Suddenly she was terrified by the size of her car. Sam's legs had already been cramped under the dashboard. 'Oh, God, Sam! Are you injured?'

'No. Just stuck. I'll have to get out your side, Kate. We'd better move. There are a lot of people out there who are going to need our help.'

There were already dazed people, moving between the crashed vehicles. Vehicles behind them on the motorway had managed to stop, before becoming further casualties, and Kate could see people frantically signalling to warn oncoming traffic of the disaster. She gazed around the scene. The lorry was tipped over on its side, several hundred yards ahead of where Kate's Mini had come to rest on the verge. The crumpled blue hatchback lay against the lorry's rear, the hooter blaring.

Ahead of the lorry the black car that had caused all the mayhem was on its roof with clouds of steam emanating from between the front wheels. The motorbike lay on its side, its rider sprawled, unmoving, some distance away. Bewildered and bleeding people were climbing shakily out of the green minibus. Another two vehicles had collided near the central reservation and the van had stopped up ahead. Kate couldn't see if it was damaged.

'Where do we start?' Kate's voice was agonised. Already she could hear the screams and wails of injured and frightened people.

Sam waved to signal some uninjured people, running towards them.

'I'm a doctor,' he shouted, 'and Kate here's an experienced emergency nurse. Are there any other medical people here?'

'I've got first-aid training.' A woman wearing a

pale grey raincoat, stepped forward. A small crowd was beginning to gather.

'I've called the emergency services.' A man waved a cellphone. 'They're on their way.'

'What did you tell them?'

'That there's been an accident and where it was.'

'Get back to them,' Sam ordered. 'Make sure they understand how many vehicles are involved. We need multiple ambulances, fire service, helicopters if they're available.' He turned to the woman in the grey raincoat.

'Take someone with you and check everybody you find,' Sam instructed. 'But don't move them. If they're bleeding heavily or not breathing call me or Kate immediately.' He raised his voice. 'Someone make sure the ignition in any vehicle is switched off and any cigarettes extinguished. You others can take care of the people with minor injuries. Bring them to this point and keep them as warm as possible. Kate, grab your kit. We'll have to try and assess who needs treatment first.'

Sam was moving as he spoke and was now near the car that had gone into the back of the overturned lorry. Kate put down her emergency kit beside him, then fumbled for the key.

'Take an airway and collar with you. Check the other vehicles.' Sam took his hand away from the unconscious driver's neck, then moved rapidly around the car. The female passenger was slumped forward, the crushed side of her head resting on the window. Her eyes were open and unseeing. Sam took his hand away from her neck, shaking his head, his expression grim as he moved back to the driver. He grabbed an airway and a stethoscope from Kate's kit as she finally got it open. Kate added some gauze pads and gloves to her own items and then ran.

Someone was waving frantically for help from the car nearest the central reservation. Vehicles on the other side of the motorway were now stopping as well, with more people rushing to offer help or simply watch.

Kate ran past the sprawled figure wearing a bike helmet. She could hear his loud groaning so knew he was at least breathing. 'Don't try to move him,' she warned the people around. 'I'll be back in a minute.' The woman she ran towards had a badly gashed forehead, but it was the laceration on her arm that needed more urgent attention. Arterial blood was pumping from it at an alarming rate, but the woman was resisting the attempts of a helper to get her to sit down.

'My kids,' she kept repeating. 'My kids are still in the car.'

Kate was pulling on her surgical gloves as she arrived by the woman's side. She took a gauze pad and held it over the site of the arterial bleed.

'They're being seen to,' she told her patient. Several people were around the silver station wagon and Kate could hear the wails of terrified children. At least they were alive. The shattered windscreen told another story and Kate glanced only quickly towards the crumpled figure that must have gone through it. The woman in the grey raincoat had her cheek near the mouth of the victim, feeling for breath movement, and her hand on his neck, feeling for a pulse. She looked up and shook her head at Kate, her face shocked. Kate nodded, the message received. She turned back quickly to the woman beside her.

'I'm Kate Campbell,' she told her. 'I'm a nurse. What's your name?'

'Jenny. My kids. Oh, God, my head hurts.' The woman swayed and Kate took her weight with her supporting arm as she helped her sit and then lie down.

A shout for help came from people near the motorbike rider. 'He's stopped breathing! Help! Someone, come quickly!'

Kate waved to a man nearby. 'Come here, will you, please? Keep pressure on this pad. Here...like this.' Kate took the man's hand and positioned it over the gauze pad. 'Don't let go—it's an arterial bleed. I'll be back in a minute, Jenny.'

Kate ran to the motorcyclist. She could see that Sam had the driver out of the car behind the lorry and was covering him with coats that people were holding out. New cries for help were now coming from people around the black car, which lay on its roof in front of the lorry, and someone was shouting from inside the green minibus. Hooters were still blaring but as Kate crouched beside her new patient she could hear a background wail of distant sirens. Help was arriving and not a moment too soon.

The man was still breathing, but not well. The hiccuping sounds were irregular and Kate could see the effort being made as she loosened the leather jacket and shirt to reveal the desperate abdominal jerks. The paramedics arrived as Kate inserted an airway carefully.

'Support his head there, love,' one told her calmly. 'We'll get this helmet off and a collar on. Is he the most urgent one for evacuation?'

'I don't know,' Kate said worriedly. 'I've only

seen two people. I'm with a doctor—Sam. Dr Marshall. He's over there.' Kate pointed behind the lorry. 'No, he's gone!' Kate turned but couldn't spot Sam. The paramedics were already lifting their patient onto a stretcher. 'Let's get an IV line in,' one said.

More sirens wailed and lights flashed as emergency ambulance, fire service and police vehicles rolled in. Traffic had been halted in both directions and the daylight was fading fast as the rain became heavier. The noise seemed deafening but Kate could still hear the chopping sound of an approaching helicopter. The bright orange machine hovered near the lorry, checking the field as a landing area. Powerful lights were coming on from the emergency vehicles and the teams of people were silhouetted against a halo of raindrops.

Most people seemed to be moving purposefully, but dotted around were the humps of dazed people, sitting or standing, some with blankets now draped around their shoulders. Television crews had materialised with unseemly speed and added to the general confusion.

Kate felt as though she had stepped into a nightmare. She wasn't sure what she should do next. She'd said she'd go back to Jenny but the woman had vanished. The crumpled figure near the front of her car was shrouded with a blanket and someone was lifting a child from the back seat. Kate felt the need to run—to offer help wherever it was needed—but she hesitated. Too many people and too much happening at once made it difficult to focus on a priority. A squeeze on Kate's arm felt instantly reassuring, the familiar voice a welcome focus.

'Kate, can you come with me? I need some help.'

She followed Sam at a run, relief washing over her. Sam's confidence was contagious. She could cope with anything with him at her side—even the driver who had caused this carnage.

He lay in his car against the heavily dented roof. Firemen were using heavy-duty cutting gear to remove the crumpled doorframe.

'Squeeze the IV bag,' Sam instructed Kate. 'We're not getting fluids in fast enough. He's losing blood fast—probably from a ruptured spleen. He's also hypoxic and very agitated. He's already pulled the IV line out twice. I'm going to try and get another one in now.'

'Why is he hypoxic?' Kate asked. She had to speak loudly over the constant groaning of the victim and the shouted orders of the fire crew. She dodged the flailing arms of her patient and gripped the soft plastic bag of haemacell, squeezing it to force the fluid though the IV line at a faster pace.

'There are a few broken ribs,' Sam call back, ripping open packages a paramedic was handing him, 'but I don't think they've done the damage. He smells of alcohol—may have vomited and aspirated some of it. We don't know what's going on with his legs yet.' Sam strapped down the cannula he had managed to insert into the man's arm and then stepped back as the firemen lifted the door section clear. They moved in again swiftly to examine the base of the crumpled steering-wheel, which was trapping the legs of the victim. The sound of their cutting equipment precluded any conversation but it seemed only a short time before the steering wheel was also removed.

'OK. We're clear,' someone shouted.

'Let's get him out. Have you got his head, Kate?'

The groans of the injured man escalated into hoarse screaming as they lifted him.

'Hold on!' It was Sam who shouted. 'Stop!'

'We're still caught somewhere.'

'It's his foot!' The fireman cursed as he shone a torch into the vehicle. 'It's caught right in the bloody engine. How the hell are we going to get into that?'

'Looks crushed to me.' The paramedic's head filled the space Kate was trying to peer into.

Sam edged in quickly. 'Move that torch a bit to the right. There's been some heavy blood loss. Looks like a partial amputation. How long to cut him free?'

The fire chief's voice was grim. 'Could be a while.'

'We haven't got a while,' Sam snapped. 'This bloke's going off fast. Is that medivac helicopter back yet?'

'Yes.'

'See if they've got an emergency amputation kit.'

A paramedic ran towards the helicopter, stooping as he neared the slowly rotating blades. Sam was cutting away what was left of the victim's trousers. 'Check his BP for me, Kate.'

Kate struggled to keep a stethoscope against the moving arm. 'Can you hold him, please?' she asked one of the fire crew.

'Take it easy, mate,' Sam called loudly. 'We're only trying to help you.'

If anything, the man's struggles became stronger at the sound of Sam's voice. There was no room for any more people to hold him.

'BP's eighty over forty-five, Sam, and the pulse is one-twenty.' She saw Sam's decisive nod.

'Draw up some lignocaine, Kate. Forty to 50 ml. We can't give him any IV narcotics until we get his BP up. It'll have to be local. Keep shoving that IV fluid in.' Sam stripped off a bloodied pair of gloves and pulled on some clean ones as the paramedic un-tied the strings on a green canvas roll and opened it. Kate suppressed a shudder at the sight of the mini-ature hacksaw that occupied the prominent middle pocket of the kit.

'We can't get near the joint so we'll have to go for a below-knee amputation,' Sam stated calmly. 'I'll go as low as possible and the orthopaedic guys can tidy up later. Our priority is to get him out of here and into hospital.'

Kate handed him a syringe of local anaesthetic and began to draw up another.

'Can we get some more light in here, please?'

A police officer, holding a powerful hand-held lamp, moved closer and a doctor from the flying squad ran towards Sam.

'We've just got that serious head injury away. Glasgow coma scale of three. Doesn't look good.' She peered over Sam's shoulder. 'Are you going to take the foot off?'

'We've got no choice. The bloke's going to die if we hang about any longer. Can you tighten that tour-niquet a bit more? I'm going for a lignocaine block.' Sam began injecting the large amount of local in a line below the level of the tourniquet. Kate took the empty syringe and handed him the second one. Sam then reached for a scalpel and cut deeply into the flesh at the back of the victim's leg.

'That's the Achilles tendon,' Kate heard him mutter. 'Right. Hand me that hacksaw...ta.'

Kate concentrated on her own tasks, replacing the bag of IV fluid and continuing to squeeze the much-needed volume back into the man's circulation. She held his oxygen mask in place with her other hand and tried to block out the sound of the saw. She failed miserably, despite the agonised groans the victim emitted. At least it was over quickly.

'Pressure bandage,' Sam instructed. 'Let's get this show on the road.'

The scene changed with dramatic swiftness. Kate stepped aside as the paramedics moved their patient onto a stretcher and then ran with him to the waiting helicopter. The doctor from the flying squad went with them.

Kate began to clear up their equipment. Sam disappeared but came back within a few minutes. He looked exhausted but he gazed at Kate with concern.

'Are you OK, love?' he queried gently.

Kate smiled shakily and nodded. As if anyone could be OK after what they had just experienced.

'Everybody's evacuated,' Sam told her. 'The police are mapping the scene and would like a statement from you if you're up to it.'

'Of course.' Kate followed Sam to the huge police van which had become the control centre for the disaster scene. Several tow trucks were here now and she noted that one lane had been cleared and a slow-moving line of traffic was being flagged through. By the time Kate had completed her interview several of the wrecks had been removed and the attention of the police was on removal of the two fatalities. Kate could see that a tow truck had attached a hook to the

front of her Mini and was lifting it clear of the deep
rut in which it was stuck.

'Could have lifted it out myself,' the man told
Kate with a cheeky grin. 'Who drives a matchbox
like that these days?'

'It's very economic,' Kate told him firmly. She
had retrieved her keys from her emergency kit and
jangled them hopefully. 'Do you reckon it'll still
go?'

'You've got a good-sized dent on the passenger
door. I could tow it in for you. I'm sure you could
get a ride with the cops.'

'I'd rather have my car.' Kate smiled triumphantly
as the engine turned over on her first try. She drove
a little way, tested the brakes and then reversed.
'Seems to be fine,' she reported.

Sam came over as Kate stopped. 'Are you sure
you want to go on? Look at us!'

'We'll need to find somewhere to clean up and get
changed,' Kate agreed. She eyed Sam's sodden and
bloodstained clothing. 'Do I look as bad as you?'

'Worse.' Sam smiled. 'We'd frighten the life out
of your mother like this.'

'There's a good B&B not far up the road.' The
tow truck driver finished loading his equipment.
'Take the next turnoff, then the first on the right and
it's a couple of miles up the road. Mrs Denver, the
lady is. You could get a wash even if you didn't
stay.'

They left the flashing lights still advertising an
emergency behind them and followed the driver's directions. Off the motorway and onto a narrow country road, the dark and the silence of the evening made
them feel as though the whole experience had been

unreal. Kate could feel the adrenaline in her system dissipate rapidly and she began to shiver. By the time they pulled up outside the old house and the sign advertising a vacancy for B&B her teeth were chattering.

'Go and explain the situation,' Sam advised. 'I'll fish out our bags so we can get a clean change of clothes.'

The B&B's proprietor was initially horrified at Kate's appearance but then became very concerned, on hearing the story.

'Of course, you must have a shower. You're frozen, you poor dear. There's oodles of hot water. Would you like one room or two?'

Kate glanced back through the main entrance. Sam was shutting the door of the Mini with his foot, a bag in each hand.

'One's fine,' she said. It wasn't as if they were planning to stay the night.

'I'll rustle up some dinner while you both clean up.' Mrs Denver clicked her tongue as she shook her head. 'I must go and put the television on—it must be all on the news.'

Kate nodded wearily. She was still shivering but, strangely, didn't feel cold any more.

'Delayed reaction,' Sam told her. 'It was a pretty stressful situation. You coped with it brilliantly.' He put the bags on the bed in the room to which Mrs Denver had shown them, then opened the door to the adjoining bathroom. 'Come on, a hot shower will do you good.' He reached in and turned on the water.

Kate pulled off her sweater but her fingers were shaking too much to undo her buttons. Sam deftly took over the task and then undid the fastening on her jeans.

'I'll leave you to it,' he said cheerfully. 'The water's nice and hot.'

'Don't go, Sam. Please? I don't think I want to be alone just yet.'

'No problem.' Sam eased off his own wet pullover. 'I'll get these things off. A dry towel will be a lot warmer.'

Kate stepped into the shower but didn't pull the door shut. It would separate her too far from Sam and she desperately needed the comfort of his presence right now.

'You can share my shower,' she offered shyly.

The draining of the adrenaline which had sustained Kate through the prolonged trauma of the emergency had left her feeling peculiarly vulnerable. The nameless fear that had crowded in on her emotions also drained away when Sam stepped into the shower cubicle with her. His sheer size overwhelmed her and his warmth and familiarity comforted her, but his proximity and nakedness provoked a desire that shocked her. Sam followed her startled gaze down his body as he reached for the soap.

'I'm always like that when I'm around you, Katy. It's a bit of a problem.' But his smile was gentle. 'Don't worry. You're in control.' He worked up a lather in his hands. 'Turn around. I'll wash your back.'

Kate let the welcome warmth of the water rain down on her face as she felt Sam's hands move up and down her back and over her shoulders. She moved back deliberately, knowing his soapy hands would slip past her armpits and onto her breasts.

When she gasped at the contact his hands retreated instantly.

'No...don't stop.' Kate twisted and her arms went around Sam's neck. 'Please don't stop.'

Sam's lips closed over hers. The shower pelted their faces and Kate was aware of the trickles of moisture as Sam pulled away.

'Are you sure, Katy? Are you sure that you're ready?'

Kate reached for the soap and rubbed it on her hands. She reached around Sam's body, running her hands down his back, onto the flat hardness of his buttocks then around to a new hardness—one which had once been a symbol of humiliation and betrayal but one that was now desperately exciting. Sam groaned in delight and Kate had never felt more sure of anything. She felt in control. Sam's lips and tongue only answered the unspoken and urgent request of her own.

Even as Sam lifted her she still felt safe, wrapping her legs around him and drawing him in of her own volition. When her control was surrendered it was also voluntary, a breaking of a final barrier that let Kate finally understand and experience the magic of passion and release.

If Mrs Denver had been worried by the amount of hot water being used by her guests, she was more concerned at the length of time it took them to appear for the dinner she'd promised. Finally she tapped gently on their door and, getting no response, opened it a little. Her guests were on the bed, a duvet loosely covering the closely entwined bodies. They were both fast asleep. Mrs Denver closed the door with a smile. From what she'd seen on television, she had a couple of heroic people on her hands. If that was the way they chose to deal with the aftermath of the stress then that was just fine by her.

She had seen the contented smile on Kate's face as she slept in the close embrace of the foreigner's arms. Whatever they had together, those two, it looked like something to be envied. Mrs Denver sighed wistfully and went to turn off her oven.

CHAPTER NINE

'I CAN'T believe how long it's got!' The hairdresser fluffed out Kate's newly washed curls. Without the usual application of mousse, Kate was also astonished at the wealth of hair she had accumulated.

'How long is it since you had it cut?'

'Must be three months,' Kate admitted. 'Or maybe even four. I lost track of time.'

The last three weeks had certainly passed in a blur, an ecstatic whirlwind of passion that had only left Kate eager for more. Even this time in the hair salon was making Kate tense with impatience. It was simply time away from Sam, time away from her lover. Kate felt the tingle sweep through her at the mere word. She'd never had a lover before. She would never want another one. Sam was perfect. He was—

'Sorry?' With some effort Kate dragged her thoughts back to the girl, standing behind her.

'I said I might need some hedge clippers. We've got a lot of hair to get rid of.'

'Oh, I don't want it cut off,' Kate instructed hurriedly. 'Just a bit of shaping around my face. And I was thinking of doing something with the colour.' Kate found herself blushing at the incredulous expression of her hairdresser. 'Nothing too drastic, though, please, Shelley.'

The hairdresser pulled herself together. 'Good for you, Kate. Time for a change.' She ran her fingers through Kate's hair again, suddenly professional. 'You've got some natural blonde highlights. Why don't we bring them out with some light frosting?'

'How long would it take?' Kate asked dubiously. Sam would be waiting back at her apartment. He probably had dinner ready. His speciality—take-aways. He might have the wine poured...the quilt turned back on the bed. Kate almost groaned out loud.

'It shouldn't take more than an hour or so,' Shelley told her. 'It would look dead brilliant.'

'OK,' Kate tried to sound enthusiastic. It was only an hour and maybe Sam had been held up in Emergency after her shift had finished. He often was. 'But let's get on with it,' she pleaded. 'I don't want to be late home.'

Even work was a distraction these days. It was fine in the face of an emergency. Both Kate and Sam could forget the electricity between them and become totally professional. But the minor cases—and worse, the quiet times—were a definite strain. Sam seemed to delight in the difficulty they had in keeping their hands off each other. Any excuse to stand close enough for their hips to touch, to brush her skin when reaching for an instrument or, best of all, a ten minute opportunity to escape and hold hands—or more—in the little park was taken with relish.

Most of the time, however, their communication was in eye contact, but that had been intense enough for everybody in the department to know exactly what was going on.

Kate grimaced at her reflection in the salon mirror. The tight plastic covering on her head was hideous and she winced as Shelley snagged tiny locks of hair and dragged them through the covering with the aid of a crochet hook.

'This had better be worth it,' she muttered. 'Ouch!'

Kate had to admit it was worth it as she gazed at the finished creation an hour later. Curls softly framed her face and bounced just below collar length when she swung her head. The glint of the highlights accentuated the sheer femininity of the casual style. Kate loved it. Shelley loved it. And Sam was more enthusiastic than either of them.

'You look like you've just had a month on Bondi Beach,' he told Kate. 'I can just imagine you, lying on the white sand—in a little string bikini! Come here, sheila,' he growled. 'I'm going to mess up that expensive new hairdo for you.'

The Indian meals Sam had warming in the oven had dried to unidentifiable mounds by the time he remembered them. They both found the sight highly amusing. It wouldn't be difficult to find a restaurant open, even at this late hour, and sleep was a luxury neither of them seemed to need too much of these days.

The expensive new hairdo caused a minor sensation when Kate arrived for work the next morning. Jude demanded to know the name of Kate's stylist and salon—it was exactly how she wanted her own hair. When Kate turned up two mornings later, wearing a new mohair jersey that was a palette for every colour of the rainbow, it was Margo's turn to covet her new look.

'Don't you think it's a bit much?' Kate eyed the garment as she removed it.

'I love it,' Margo repeated firmly. 'And it really

suits you. Those greys and browns you always used to wear were disgusting!'

Kate smiled. A month ago a comment like that would have only reached her ears when she was hidden in the shower cubicle. Not only could Margo say it to her face but Kate could nod embarrassed agreement.

'So where did you find it?'

'Sam insisted on buying it for me,' Kate admitted reluctantly. 'He found it when we were wandering around Covent Garden yesterday.'

'It looks like something he'd choose.' Margo nodded.

'I knew it was a bit much!' Kate folded the soft, bright wool and tucked it into her locker.

'He's not, though, is he?' Margo raised an eyebrow. 'I must say I rather envy you, Kate.'

Kate hid her expression as she slipped her uniform over her head. Gorgeous, popular Margo—envying her! It was really quite unbelievable how much her life had changed. But Kate didn't want the pace of change to continue. She would like to stop the clock exactly where they were at this moment. At least for a while—until she could get used to things.

'It's not that much longer until he goes back to Australia, is it?'

Kate was pinning on her watch. She felt a chill spread through her. 'About six weeks, I guess,' she said casually. 'I'm not really sure.' She shut her locker door with a bang as she told the lie. She knew exactly. And it wasn't six weeks. It was only five. In fact, it was only four weeks and five days now, and Sam had still not said anything of his immediate plans on finishing at St Matthew's. It wasn't a subject

Kate felt she could initiate. She twisted her locker key with a frown. Her life had been stable for so many years.

The changes had brought astonishing happiness but the prospect of more change was frightening. What she had now was too good to be true. A push in the wrong direction could be enough to shatter the illusion. She trusted Sam and how he felt about her, but he was an adventurer. Adventurers, by and large, did not favour permanence and Kate didn't want to settle for anything less. It was safer not to bring the subject out in the open—at least, not before it became absolutely necessary.

The loud buzz of conversation within the department signalled a quiet spell for the staff change-over. Kate was surprised to find Sam with his arms around Louise. Jeff was smiling at them both. Sam released Louise, who was looking unusually flustered.

'Louise is going to be the new junior consultant here,' Sam informed Kate.

'Oh, congratulations!' Kate smiled. 'That's great!'

Louise returned her smile. 'Isn't it? I'm thrilled. I just hope I can cope.'

'With Kate around, you can cope with anything,' Jeff assured her.

'I can vouch for that,' Sam agreed. 'Hey, Katy, I called the hospital at Swindon this morning. Brigid Llewellyn has come out of her coma. She's doing really well.'

'That's amazing,' Kate exclaimed. 'I expected her to be the third fatality.'

'You and everybody else,' Sam nodded.

They had kept in touch with the hospital over the last few weeks. Sam had been determined to find out everything he could about the accident victims. Kate had been surprised at his level of interest.

'They're not just isolated patients,' he had explained. 'They've all got families, and trauma has such a far-reaching effect. It's part of what appeals to me about the flying doctor service. You get to know the small communities and you can follow up the ripple effect as well. It's just not possible in big cities.'

Kate had to agree. It had been fascinating, all the details Sam had unearthed. Jenny, the woman with the arterial bleed, had been discharged within days. Her children had only had minor injuries and the newborn baby had been unscathed, thanks to the car-seat into which he had been strapped. It had been Jenny's husband who had been killed instantly, having gone through the windscreen of the car. He'd been the only occupant not wearing a seat belt. The trip had been a visit to let the grandparents see the new addition to the family. Now all their lives had been changed irrevocably.

'At least they still have their mother,' Sam had reminded Kate. 'Thanks to you.'

The rider of the motorbike had been in Intensive Care for ten days but was now on the road to recovery. The driver of the black car who had caused the accident was due for further surgery. He would be left permanently disabled, scarred physically and emotionally by his careless actions. He would also be facing prosecution as soon as his condition allowed.

The woman with the serious head injuries, Brigid Llewellyn, had been the final patient Sam had been following up. She'd been the only passenger in the green minibus to receive serious injuries—and that had been because she'd decided to change seats. Almost standing when the bus had swerved away from the motor bike, she had been hurled forward into the dashboard. Brigid also had a family. Her parents, husband and teenage children had been keeping vigil in the intensive care unit throughout the duration of her coma. Kate knew that Sam would be sharing their pleasure and relief at her improvement.

She watched him now, taking delight in the reaction of other staff members as he relayed the news of Louise's appointment. He could involve himself so easily in the lives of other people and could evoke a trust and affection that was astounding. Kate wondered yet again why she'd been singled out for a special relationship. Why had he been prepared to persevere when other choices would have been so easy? Whatever the reason, she could only feel incredibly lucky—and grateful. S.A. Marshall must have touched and changed many lives in his thirty-seven years, but Kate felt that surely none had been as profoundly changed as her own.

'This calls for a big party!' Sam was telling Joe and Margo.

'So you're almost out of a job, then?' Margo sounded disappointed.

'As of now, officially,' Sam agreed with a grin. 'You'll have to put up with me, pottering about for a few more weeks, but I'm heading back on the...'

Kate didn't hear the rest of Sam's sentence because of a commotion in Reception. The patient, a young woman, was walking but was very distressed.

'Help me! Help me!' she was repeating hoarsely.

Sam and Kate assisted her into the resuscitation area. Louise was already holding the oxygen equipment.

'She's got asthma,' Sam told her tersely. 'Kate, draw up 6 mg adrenaline and 6 ml IV Ventolin.' He pulled on a pair of gloves. 'And a 2 mg bolus of salbutamol, ta.'

Joe was attaching ECG leads as Sam inserted an IV cannula. Margo was removing the patient's clothing a few minutes later when Jeff came into the area.

'Status asthmaticus,' Sam informed the senior consultant. 'Unresponsive so far.'

Louise had switched to an ambu bag to assist the patient's breathing. She kept up a constant stream of verbal encouragement and reassurance. Kate provided a needle for Jeff, who performed an arterial stab in the patient's groin to get a blood-gas reading. Then she set up the salbutamol infusion Sam had requested. Jeff had his stethoscope on the patient's chest, repeatedly tapping her ribs. He looked up at Sam.

'Let's give her another 2 mg salbutamol.'

'She's already had six.'

Jeff nodded. 'We're not getting much of a response yet, though.'

The minutes ticked by. Their patient became less responsive. Louise was shouting now, trying to get her to open her eyes.

'How long since she came in?'

Kate glanced at the clock. 'Twenty minutes.'

The intensive care registrar arrived. Kate watched him examine their patient, who was now unconscious.

'We'll have to ventilate her,' he announced. Kate

reached for an endotracheal tube. It felt as if they were losing. Ventilating a severe asthmatic was avoided if at all possible. It was so much easier to get air in than out and a popped lung was a complication nobody wanted.

'Watch the clock,' the registrar instructed Louise. 'Keep your hand off the bag and don't give her another one for twenty seconds.' He moved to the phone to let the unit know he was bringing the patient up. 'Set up a salbutamol infusion,' Kate heard him instruct. 'She's coming up paralysed and sedated.'

Kate watched her being transferred. She knew that she would know her name and condition by the end of the day. She would probably know about her family and her entire medical history by then as well if Sam had anything to do with it.

The days slipped by. The staff gathering at the pub to celebrate Louise's appointment was as enjoyable as the one the following week to celebrate Joe's birthday. It was the first time anyone had even known when Joe's birthday was.

It had been Sam who had brought the department together so closely, Kate decided, watching him pass around packets of his favourite Marmite-flavoured crisps. What was going to happen when he left? Kate didn't want to think about it. Sam seemed as happy as she was to live for the present. Her increasing niggles of apprehension only occurred when she wasn't exclusively in his company and they would just have to be subdued. Work was wonderful but not as good as a day off when it coincided with one for Sam. That luxury was unfortunately becoming less frequent.

'I'd better work a bit harder,' Sam had joked. 'I need a good reference from Jeff when I leave.'

They'd had an afternoon together the day after Joe's birthday celebration. The weather had tempted them out for a walk and they'd ended up sitting on the grass on Primrose Hill. There were several dogs being walked but Sam's attention was focused on Kate. He stared at her intently for a long moment then smiled lazily.

'So, tell me about kung fu,' he said.

'Judo.' The correction was automatic but Kate returned the smile. 'What do you want to know?'

'Why do you do it? Do you have some repressed violent tendencies I should know about?'

Kate laughed. 'It's a good way to stay fit. I used to enjoy the challenge of competitions.' She paused reflectively. 'I wouldn't mind trying something else now, though.'

'Like what?'

'I'd quite like…' Kate paused again, suddenly shy. 'I'd like to learn to ride a horse,' she finished abruptly.

'Yeah? Good on you.' Sam's eyes crinkled in amusement. 'But why not get really adventurous? You could learn to ride a camel.'

'Oh, sure. Where would I find a camel stables around here?'

'There're plenty of camels in the outback. Maybe I'll get you one for your birthday. When is your birthday?'

'First of October,' Kate responded, but her thoughts were on the implications of Sam's idle comment. Did he assume she would be in the outback at some point? Did he intend to invite her to join him? Or was it simply a reflection of Sam's casual attitude and confidence that life would sort itself out according to his preferences?

'I'd better stick to judo, I think.'

'You haven't told me much about it.' Sam seemed happy to change the subject. 'What was that move you used on me that nearly broke my back?'

'That was a *Makikomi* with a sort of *Tai-otoshi* leg movement.'

'That means a lot.'

'A winding throw,' Kate explained. 'You can generate a lot of power by a rotational movement. I knew you were a lot bigger than me. And I knocked you off balance with my foot at the same time. Want me to show you?'

'No.' Sam laughed. 'Thanks, anyway. Show me something else. Something with less potential for serious injury.'

'OK. Stand up, then. Now, put both your hands around my neck—like you were planning to strangle me.'

Sam's hands loosely enfolded Kate's neck. She took hold of his forearms.

'Now, I put my foot here.' Kate leaned back and placed the sole of her foot against Sam's stomach. 'The idea is that I drop on the spot, which tips you over my head to land on your back.'

'I'm ready.' Sam was grinning broadly.

Kate dropped her body weight suddenly but Sam was ready for it. Instead of pivoting over her head, Sam remained standing as her leg collapsed, then he fell directly on top of her. He was still grinning.

'I like this move.'

'That's not the way it's supposed to happen.' Kate gratefully took a breath as Sam took his weight on his elbows.

'I think it's a vast improvement.' Sam bent his head and kissed Kate's lips lingeringly. He raised his head again and gazed at her steadily, his face only inches from hers.

Kate was trapped. It was a situation that could, and until very recently would, have caused her to panic. Instead, she could feel the trust she had in Sam enfold her. She felt safe. And so happy it threatened to overwhelm her. The moment was so perfect Kate wanted nothing to change—ever. Her hands went behind Sam's head, her fingers laced in the tousled curls as she drew his lips back to hers.

'You're right,' she murmured. 'It is a vast improvement.'

Another week slipped by with their only time together measured in a few short hours, usually late in the day. It was so easy to spend that time, making love, eating out or simply falling asleep together in front of the television. Kate tried to use the time she had on her own constructively but found herself, more often than not, merely daydreaming. Filling in time until she could be with Sam again.

'Have you got a spare aerogram?' he asked one evening. 'I need to write to my mother. Have you written to yours yet?'

'No, I meant to this evening but I was too busy, tidying up. Has anyone ever told you you're a slob? I thought you told me you were house-trained.'

'I think I said almost house-trained. Maybe I

should have said hospital-trained. I tend to forget at home. You'll have to talk to my mum about it.' Sam yawned hugely and then grinned. 'At least you'll have one thing in common.'

Kate was silent for a moment. There was that casual assumption again that she would continue to be a part of Sam's life when he returned to Australia. They were just dropped into the conversation, almost as though they were bait. But Kate wasn't going to bite. Not yet. If he wanted a casual approach then two could play at that game.

'It'll be more than you had in common with my mother,' she reminded him. 'She looked as though you'd arrived from an alien planet when we finally turned up.'

'We should have rung to tell her about the hold-up. It was no wonder she was a bit upset.'

'Dazed, more like. And you kept reeling off all those statistics about the flying doctors.'

'You needed some time to feel comfortable together again. I was providing a distraction,' Sam said with satisfaction. 'It worked, didn't it?'

'It was fascinating,' Kate assured him. 'And, yes, it helped a lot, having something neutral to discuss. I think there's something there we'll be able to build on. It's a bit difficult to know where to start, though. That's why it's taking me so long to write that letter.' Kate sighed, then looked at Sam with interest. 'Does the flying doctor service really cover seven million square kilometres?'

'Near enough.'

'And the planes are really that sophisticated?'

Sam nodded. 'Flying emergency departments. The base I'm going to has Beechcraft King Air planes.

Turbo props, satellite navigation systems—amazing stuff.' He eyed Kate. 'I meant what I said about the flight nurses, too. Most evacuations don't carry a doctor. The nurses have all the responsibility. They need to run a lot of the remote field clinics and radio consultations as well. It needs a special breed. You'd be perfect, Kate.'

'It does sound exciting,' Kate admitted. 'Did they ask you to drum up some extra recruits while you were over here?'

'No, that was all my own idea.' Sam grinned proudly. 'But I'm sure the blokes in administration will be delighted.'

'I doubt it. I wouldn't have the obstetric skills needed.'

'You could get them easily enough. I can recommend an advanced training sabbatical.' Sam reached for Kate and pulled her towards him. 'You get to meet the nicest people.' He kissed her several times. 'Then, again,' he murmured huskily, 'I don't think I should recommend it at all. Could be dangerous.'

'Could be,' agreed Kate. 'Now, don't you think I should get on with that letter to my mother?'

'What letter?'

Kate laughed and snuggled deeper into Sam's embrace. 'Never mind. Where were we?'

There was plenty of time to write the letter to her mother the following evening. Even though the task was difficult it provided a welcome distraction from the increasing apprehension Kate was experiencing. She was sure Sam was hiding something. He'd deliberately avoided her at work that day, disappeared completely during his lunch-break, and had seemed disconcerted when Kate had appeared in his office at the end of her shift.

'You go home without me, Katy. I've got something to see to in town.'

'You had something to see to in town yesterday!'

'Mmm. It needs finishing off.'

'I'll come with you.'

'No, that's OK. I know where I'm going.'

'Where *are* you going?' Kate hadn't been able to help sounding suspicious.

'Nowhere in particular.' Sam had seemed suddenly very interested in the paperwork he'd been shuffling.

'Fine. I'll see you at home, then.' Kate had been bothered by Sam's evasiveness. Her tone had been tentative but Sam's cheerful grin and wave had done nothing to reassure her.

There was plenty to occupy her at her apartment. She counted six pairs of Sam's socks, which she had to unravel, before putting them into the laundry bag. He's a slob, she told herself. How could anybody live with someone so untidy? Even if his untidiness couldn't be excused by the fact that he was living out of a backpack, Kate couldn't bring herself to feel annoyed. Picking up dirty socks was a small price to pay for the joy his company provided. And it was only two weeks until she'd have her apartment to herself again. She knew the tidiness would be unbearably lonely.

Sam arrived home, looking very pleased with himself.

'All sorted out, then?'

'Almost. There's a fair bit to do.'

'I'm sure there is.' Kate's heart rate increased. She

was running out of time and Sam seemed to have no intention of confiding his plans. 'You're due to finish on the fourteenth aren't you?'

'That's right.' Sam poked his finger into the pot Kate was stirring and then licked it. 'Delicious! Shall I get some plates?'

Kate ignored the query. 'Have you got any plans for what you're going to do?'

'A few. I haven't finalised anything yet.'

Kate stirred the pot more vigorously and tried to match Sam's casual tone. 'I've got some leave due. I've asked for a week, starting on the fifteenth. I thought perhaps you'd like to go somewhere. Maybe Scotland?' Kate blinked hard. 'I thought it might be nice to spend a few days together before you head back home.'

Sam was collecting the plates. 'Not a bad idea, Kate. I'll give it some thought.'

The noncommittal tone made Kate swallow hard. If Sam wasn't going to take the opportunities she offered him there wasn't much more she could do. She knew perfectly well that Sam was aware of how she felt. She'd been unable to hide her best-kept secret from him. She wasn't even trying to hide her dismay at the prospect of him leaving. Her voice wobbled when she spoke again.

'Have you booked a flight back yet?'

'I'm working on it. Might have to pop into town again after work tomorrow.'

'You do intend to let me know some time, Sam?' Kate's anxiety gave her voice a sharp edge.

'You'll be the first to know,' Sam promised. He gave Kate a thoughtful stare. 'Trust me, Katy.' He continued to stare at her but frowned suddenly.

'Damn it,' he said. 'I forgot to get some wine.' He grabbed his parka from the cupboard handle over which he'd draped it. 'I'll just run down to the off-licence.'

'There's no need,' Kate protested. 'We can do without—'

But Sam had gone. With a sigh Kate turned the gas under her pot down to a low simmer and then sat to wait for Sam's return.

So he didn't want to go to Scotland with her. He obviously had other plans. Kate felt more sure than ever that he was hiding something. She'd given this man her complete trust. Was he testing it?

Or could it be that Dr S.A. Marshall really did have something he wanted to hide?

CHAPTER TEN

KATE felt the stirrings of anger.

She did her best to dampen it, trying to concentrate on her task.

'How are you feeling now, Mrs Tonkin?' Kate wrapped the BP cuff around the ample upper arm of her patient.

'Much better, thank you, dear. I'm sorry to cause so much trouble.'

'It's no trouble.' Kate pulled her stethoscope from around her neck and put in her earpieces with some relief. At least she wouldn't be aware of the whispered conversation on the other side of the cubicle curtain. She couldn't hear what it was about and she knew that it would stop the moment she appeared. This time it was between Margo and Joe. Yesterday it had been Margo and Jude, and the day before that between Sam and Jeff.

At first Kate thought she was being paranoid but the quick glances that came in her direction during the snatched conversations, and the way the other staff members all found something that they had to get on with as soon as she came near, could only mean one thing. She was the subject of their conversations.

'Your blood pressure's still normal, Mrs Tonkin,' Kate announced. 'And everything else checks out fine. Your low blood sugar is most likely to be because of the meals you've been skipping. The doctors are happy that it was the cause of your fainting.'

'So embarrassing!' her patient groaned. 'The ambulance men had to ask for assistance to lift me. You can see why I'm desperate to lose weight.'

'Starving's not the answer,' Kate said firmly. 'And it can be dangerous. That was quite a bump you got on your head when you collapsed. It's lucky you didn't do any real damage.'

'I do have rather a headache still, dear.'

'I'll get you something for it. I think we've kept you here under observation long enough. The doctors are happy for you to go home now.'

'Lovely man,' Mrs Tonkin said with feeling. 'Can I see him before I go? To say thank you?'

'I'm not sure where he is at the moment.' Kate frowned. In fact, Sam had vanished from the department an hour ago. The disappearing acts were becoming a habit and his explanations were, in Kate's opinion, pathetically evasive. 'I'll pass your message on,' she assured Mrs Tonkin as she helped her patient to her feet. This was no easy task but it didn't distract Kate from a new and firm resolution. She was going to pass on more than Mrs Tonkin's message. She was going to let Dr Marshall know that she was fed up. She wanted to know just what the hell was going on around here.

However, it was Sam who cornered Kate thirty minutes later. 'Katy, I need to talk to you.'

'You certainly do! What's going on around here, Sam?'

Sam gazed briefly around the department. 'The usual, by the look of it. Oh, someone's thrown up in cubicle two—it stinks to high heaven.'

'That's not what I mean and you know it.' Kate repressed a ridiculous urge to stamp her foot. She'd had more than enough of this cheerful evasiveness.

'I haven't got time to stop and chat, Kate. I'm late.'

'What for?'

'I've got to get out to Heathrow. It'll be a slow trip at this time of day.'

Kate's mouth dropped open. Was this her farewell? Sam was still talking and she realised she hadn't heard a word.

'So I told Lizzy I'd stay at the hotel with her tonight to make sure she's settled in.'

'Who the hell is Lizzy?'

'My oldest sister. Kate, really! You haven't listened to a word I've said.' Sam's admonishing tone was tempered by a grin. 'She's bent on shopping till she drops so I'm taking her out tomorrow to hit the high street.'

'I'll come with you,' Kate offered. 'I've got the day off.'

'No—don't do that,' Sam said quickly. His eyes slid away from Kate's. 'Ah...I'm not sure how jet-lagged she'll be.' A look of relief flashed across his features. 'There's Jeff! I must have a quick word. Bye, Katy.' Sam planted a quick kiss on her forehead. 'I'll ring you tomorrow.'

Kate turned back to the whiteboard but couldn't concentrate on the muddle of information. Just as well it was time for a shift change, she thought. She'd had enough of the department for one day. Still feeling bemused by Sam's behaviour, she turned away from the board in time to see him give Jeff a thumbs-up sign as he exited the department. Jeff had a very uncharacteristically broad grin on his face as he also watched Sam leave.

Why hadn't Sam told her his sister was arriving? And why did he seem to not want Kate to meet her? The anger Kate had been suppressing surfaced as she changed out of her uniform. It was anger heavily laced with suspicion, however, and by the time Kate emerged from the locker room it had changed character completely. The nameless fear which had haunted her for the last few weeks was with her again, but it was no longer nameless. Why was Sam so obviously hiding something, and just who was he going to meet at the airport?

On impulse, Kate ran lightly up the stairs and kept going until she was in the small office next to Jeff's which had been assigned to Sam. She went straight to the desk. It was a mess. It was littered with piles of patient reports, opened medical journals, notes scrawled on scraps of paper and two empty packets of Marmite flavoured crisps.

'House-trained, indeed!' Kate muttered. She picked up an official-looking form, lying on top of one of the heaps. It was an uncompleted form for travel insurance. Kate was astonished by the boxes already filled in, giving the applicant's full name. Sebastian Alexander Marshall. Sebastian! Kate laughed out loud. No wonder it was such a secret! She was still laughing as she replaced the form carefully. She wondered if Tommy Bragan had been laughing while his nose bled.

Kate saw the aerogram she had supplied Sam with days ago—also uncompleted. Only the address panel had been filled in. To a Mrs S.A. Marshall in Queensland, Australia.

Her amusement over Sam's given names faded instantly. Mrs S.A. Marshall. Kate sat slowly. Was this what Sam had been hiding. A *wife*?

'No!' Kate whispered the denial and then spoke aloud more firmly. 'No. I don't believe it.'

Nobody could hide something like that so well. Especially not Sam. She trusted him even if his behaviour had been odd lately. Even though he had been preoccupied and evasive, Kate had still been convinced she was at least one of his priorities. Surely his love-making had been proof of that?

But, then, what did Kate really know about relationships and trust? Sam was her first lover. She was a mere beginner in a game in which intuition told her that he must be a very experienced player. Perhaps her assumption that what they had was special enough to ensure permanence was simply naïvety on her part. Kate shook her head. She didn't believe it. Her instincts for self-protection had been finely honed over the last decade, and she had never felt in any real danger of being betrayed by Sam.

He'd instructed her to trust him and, difficult as it was right now, that was precisely what she intended to do. Maybe Mrs S.A. Marshall was an ex-wife who hadn't changed her name. Kate had never tried to pry into Sam's past relationships. Her own had cast enough of a shadow over the present. But now it was time to make sure there were no more secrets. When he rang her she would arrange for them to have some time together, some time in which they could talk. Really talk, the way Sam had warned her they would after the incident of her suspension.

As Kate began to feel calmer her vision was focused on the desk again and her eye was caught by a brightly coloured brochure, half-hidden by a medical journal. She eased it out. The photographs were idyllic, the first of a luxury launch, leaving a wake behind it as it cruised over a calm sea to the distant green humps of tropical-looking islands. The text below asked the reader to imagine what the resort would be like if this was the hotel limousine.

The pictures of the resort didn't need any imaginative embellishment, however. The grounds seemed to be one vast, sparkling swimming pool, lapping to the very edges of the hotel buildings and extending out into the sea itself, with bridged walkways to a large island covered with umbrella-shaded tables and chairs.

Kate flicked through the brochure. Hayman Island was clearly a paradise. Holidaymakers were snorkelling over the Great Barrier Reef in water as clear as glass. Some were sailing Hobie-cats, windsurfing, playing golf or tennis or working out in a health club. Others were simply lying by the pool, glasses of champagne evident. Kate sighed wistfully and turned the last page.

The fax message was tucked into the back of the brochure. It confirmed the booking of the most luxurious East Wing suite for a period of ten days, starting on the eighteenth. In five days' time! The message from hotel management finished by saying they were looking forward to welcoming Dr Marshall and his wife.

Kate's fingers seemed frozen as she fumbled to replace the fax and the brochure exactly where she'd found them. No wonder Sam had been so preoccupied. He'd had a lot to arrange. And no wonder the prospect of a week with her in Scotland had failed to attract him. Scotland might be beautiful but it couldn't compete with paradise. He might love her but she couldn't—and wouldn't want to— compete with a wife.

When the phone rang the next morning Kate ignored it. She felt terrible. The sleepless and lonely night, and the emotional anguish she'd experienced, had left her feeling totally drained and had given her a pounding headache. She knew who was ringing and she had no intention of speaking to him. He could just join the club. His name could be added to the list of people Kate had trusted and then been betrayed by. Only this time the pain was worse. It was unbearable.

How could he have done it? How could he have worked so long and hard to win her trust and her love in order to shatter it? Her instincts told her that Sam was simply not capable of such cruelty, but her instincts surely had to surrender in the face of such irrefutable facts. No matter how many times during the long hours alone Kate had tried to imagine an explanation, nothing even remotely believable had presented itself.

When the phone rang again a few minutes later Kate considered taking it off the hook, but then he would know she was at home and could possible turn up on the doorstep. Perhaps he would turn up with his sister in tow.

'Oh, God,' Kate muttered. It was quite likely he'd turn up anyway, whether she took the phone off the hook or not. She snatched up the receiver.

'Morning, sweetheart! I hope I didn't wake you up.'

'No. I wasn't asleep.'

'What's up? You don't sound too happy.'

Kate was silent. A conversation on the subject of why she wasn't happy couldn't be conducted over a telephone—and where on earth would she begin, anyway?

Sam's voice was a husky drawl. 'God, I missed you last night, Katy. Did you miss me?'

'I was thinking about you. Rather a lot, in fact.' Kate tried to keep her voice steady. 'I need to talk to you, Sam. Really talk.'

She could sense the hesitation on the other end of the line. 'I'm a bit tied up today, Kate. Can you meet me for dinner?'

'Why don't you come here?'

'No.' Again there was a hesitation. 'I've made a reservation, actually. We've never had a really posh dinner together, have we? Only afternoon tea. I'd really love to see you all dressed up to the nines, drinking champagne by candlelight.'

'I haven't got anything to wear to somewhere like that,' Kate replied tonelessly. The idea of a romantic dinner in an exclusive restaurant was unthinkable right now. Or was it? Perhaps it was, in fact, a perfect setting for unveiling secrets and, if necessary, saying goodbye.

'You've got the day off, haven't you?' Sam's voice was pleading. 'Go and buy the most beautiful dress you can find. I'll pay for it.'

'I'll pay for it myself, thank you.'

'So you will come, then?' His relief was obvious.

'I'll think about it.'

'Ripper! Oh, one other thing,' Sam added hurriedly. 'Make sure it's not a black dress.'

'Why?'

'Because…ah…because you only ever wore dark colours when I met you, Katy.' Sam's voice was suddenly quiet and serious. 'I don't want you ever hiding in the shadows again.'

It was amazing, the effect Sam's voice had had on her. When she hung up Kate's instincts were winning the battle again. After considerable thought, and a couple of aspirin to chase her headache away, Kate decided she would accept the dinner invitation. If nothing else, it would be a valuable lesson to discover whether or not her instincts could be trusted.

She was puzzled by Sam's direction about dress colour but slightly relieved as well. She had never suited black with her pale skin. It made her features stand out and look even sharper and more pixie-like than ever. White was equally unsuitable. It drained what little colour she did have and made her look like a ghost. But a bright rainbow hue didn't seem appropriate either.

When she saw the floor-length creation in ivory silk with a fine gold thread woven through the fabric Kate fell in love with it instantly. The strapless evening gown fell from the wired bra top in fluid folds. When she moved, the light caught the gold thread and made the whole dress shimmer. Kate had never seen anything like it. She'd never seen anything like the price either. There goes the trip to Africa, she thought sadly as she handed over her credit card.

Shelley was delighted to fit her in to wash and blow-wave her hair. Then she insisted on ringing a friend of hers who worked at a nearby beauty salon.

'Treat yourself,' she ordered Kate. 'Have a facial

and get your make-up done. It's the first time I've ever done your hair for a night out. It must be a special occasion.'

So Kate entered a beauty salon for the first time in her life. Her day was used up by the time she emerged, but the shopping and appointments had been a good distraction from her nervous anticipation of the evening ahead. She only had time to get home, feed Bartholemew and change into her dress. She had no suitable jewellery to wear and had no intention of fiddling with either her hair or make-up. The combination of expertise in the salons had made her look—and feel— transformed. When she put on her dress Kate laughed aloud.

'You shall go to the ball, Cinderella,' she told her reflection. Then her smile faded. 'But I wonder what will happen after midnight?'

Kate's taxi arrived promptly and it was a short trip to the hotel. The side-room Kate was shown to was small and dimly lit by candles. Sam was the only occupant of the room, even though there were several tables discreetly spaced from each other. None of the tables would fit more than two people. It was a room designed for romantic and intimate occasions. A silent waiter filled tall flutes with champagne and then withdrew as Sam took hold of Kate's hands and gazed at her in stunned admiration.

'Stone the crows, Katy! You must be the most gorgeous creature alive.'

'You don't look too bad yourself.' Kate's eyes took in the elegant dinner suit, the elaborate pin-tucks on the silk shirt, the black bow-tie and the silver cuff-links. In any other setting the effect would have been completely over the top. Kate smiled. Sam stood out, no matter what he wore or whatever the setting. 'It's a shame there's no one else here to admire us,' she said lightly.

'I booked all the tables,' Sam said casually. 'I wanted some privacy.'

'You booked the *whole* restaurant?'

'Not exactly. There's a private function on in their ballroom. I just got this one for us. Come and sit down, Kate. I really need to talk to you.'

Kate sat slowly, still stunned. Sam had done this just for her. He was looking at her now as though he would book the moon for her if she expressed any desire to visit it.

'I'm not sure exactly when I fell in love with you, Kate Campbell,' Sam said softly. 'At first I just wanted to know what made you seem to stand out from everybody else. I think I began to realise why when that kid threw up on Julian's shoes and you were trying so hard not to show anything on your face. I caught a glimpse of the real you, hiding in there, then.'

Kate smiled. She took a sip of her champagne, letting the bubbles explode on her tongue.

'And then!' Sam continued in an incredulous tone, '*Then* you flattened me with your kung fu and I knew I was lost.' He reached over and caught Kate's hand. 'You gave me your trust,' he said gently, 'and you let me love you. That was the most precious thing anyone has ever given me. Now I want to give you mine. But first I have a confession to make.'

Kate felt her hand stiffen in Sam's grasp but he wouldn't release it. 'I have my own secret,' Sam told her carefully. 'Nothing like yours, but one that changed my life rather dramatically and made me unsure about trusting someone again.'

'Is this about your marriage?' Kate's whisper was shaky.

'How did you know that?' Sam's stare was intense but he cleared his throat. 'Never mind. It wasn't a marriage, anyway. There I was, dressed up like a right Charlie in front of three hundred people waiting for the bride who never showed up.'

Kate gasped. 'You were *jilted*?'

'At the altar. Wonderful setting for a comedy—only nobody was laughing. Especially me.'

'Why did she do it?'

'She decided I wasn't the one for her. Apparently, she decided a block or two away from the church so she told the driver to turn around and take her home.' He squeezed Kate's hand. 'I'll tell you all the ghastly details some time. What matters at the moment is that it seemed like the ultimate betrayal at the time and I didn't think I'd ever really get over it. It's been six years now and it pales in comparison to what you've been through but maybe you can understand how I felt.'

Kate nodded. 'You never tried again?'

'I never wanted to. Until now.' Sam was now holding both Kate's hands across the narrow table. 'I never want to be apart from you, Kate. I asked you here for a very particular reason.'

'To tell me your secret?' Kate offered.

'No. I asked you here to marry me.'

'You mean to ask me to marry you?'

'No, I mean to marry me.'

Kate gave a nervous chuckle. 'Before or after dinner?'

'Before.'

Kate met the intense look Sam was giving her. 'I love you, Kate. Will you marry me? Please?'

'I love you, too, Sam,' Kate replied softly. 'You've given me a life that I couldn't imagine being without now. I could think of nothing I'd like more than to marry you. But...'

'But what?' Sam's face creased with alarm.

'But I think it might be pushing it to do it before dinner.'

Sam's characteristic grin wiped away his frown. He leaned forward. 'In that ballroom next door is about half the consultant staff of St Matthew's. More than half the emergency department staff, including Patsy. My mother and Lizzy, who flew in from Australia yesterday, and your mother, who is still looking rather dazed but is, by the way, very happy to adopt Bartholemew. The marriage celebrant is waiting in the foyer. The paperwork is all attended to. Our tickets home are booked and our honeymoon is all arranged. All you need to do is say yes.'

'And if I don't?' Kate's eyes were dancing.

'Apart from a few select people, everybody thinks they're here for my farewell bash. If you say no we'd still have a great party and I'd have a lonely holiday on the Great Barrier Reef.'

'Didn't you trust me enough to wait at the front of a church?'

Sam's smile was uncharacteristically tentative. 'I was scared to give you too much time to think about it. I couldn't bear to lose you, Kate.' His smile became a grin. 'You seem to have got the hang of sex so well I thought you might decide it would be fun to play the field a bit.'

'It's not sex I'm so keen on, Sam,' Kate replied seriously. 'It's making love. And there is only one person I'm ever going to be able to do that with. As far as I'm concerned, there's only ever been one player on the field.'

Sam sighed happily. 'I really was afraid I'd scare you off. I've been a nervous wreck for the last couple of weeks while I was setting all this up. I was sure you'd figured out what I was up to and you didn't seem too thrilled about it.'

Kate shook her head. 'I knew you were up to something but I had no idea what. That's why I came here tonight—to try and find out.'

'Well, now you know. No more secrets—ever.' Sam stood. He still held one of Kate's hands. 'Will you do me the honour of becoming my wife?'

'I'd love to.' Kate rose and stood beside Sam. 'Do you think my dress is OK?'

'Perfect. Except for one thing.' Sam fished in his pocket and produced a small box. Kate clicked it open to find a solitaire diamond, not a ring but a simple pendant on a fine, gold chain. Sam fastened it and then bent to place a gentle kiss on the back of Kate's neck.

'Now we're ready.' Sam signalled the waiters, who opened the double doors of the ballroom. Kate could see the familiar and excited faces of her colleagues as she walked in beside Sam, her arm linked through his.

'G'day!' Sam's voice caused the last pockets of conversation to cease. 'Before we get this party under way, folks, we have a little announcement to make. Kate and I are getting married.' Sam waited for the applause and exclamations to subside. 'Welcome to our wedding,' he added with a grin. 'Jeff, are you ready?'

The older consultant stepped out of the crowd and smiled at Kate fondly. 'May I have the honour of giving you away? I *am* losing you in a way.'

Sam then called for Margo, who appeared with two bouquets of flowers. She handed one to Kate and then held out a delicate matching wreath made of single white daisies. She reached up and placed it carefully on Kate's head.

'They were just lying around,' Sam whispered to Kate. 'I thought I'd pick them up in case I needed them.'

'They're perfect.' Kate smiled.

There were some hurried introductions to the representatives from Sam's family. Kate liked his mother instantly.

'Call me Susan, love,' she ordered Kate.

Kate nodded happily and greeted Lizzy, who was a female version of Sam— almost six feet tall, with the same streaked blonde hair and the tan, which Sam had now almost completely lost. She could sense that conversation with Sam's sister would be easy but she turned back quickly to his mother. 'Does your middle name start with A?'

'Yes, it does.' Susan Marshall looked puzzled. 'It's Alexandra. Sam's middle name was after me. He's Alexander.'

'I know.' Kate smiled again. Mrs S.A. Marshall. It was probably the only explanation that hadn't occurred to her. Suddenly her eyes widened and she hurried over to join Sam. He was standing before the marriage celebrant. Joe stood beside him, dressed in a matching dinner suit and clutching a ring box in his hand. He winked at Kate but she tugged urgently at Sam's sleeve.

'Hey!' she whispered. 'Are you sure you want to go through with this?'

Sam had never looked more serious. 'Why wouldn't I?'

'Because,' Kate replied solemnly, 'everybody is going to find out what your initials stand for.'

Sam laughed—a joyous roar that made everybody in the room smile and wish they could share the joke.

'I can live with it,' he whispered to Kate. 'No more secrets, remember?'

'No more secrets,' Kate repeated quietly. 'I'll never forget.'

Hand in hand, they turned to face the celebrant and an expectant hush fell over the gathering.

MILLS & BOON®

Medical Romance™

COMING NEXT MONTH

A TRUSTWORTHY MAN by Josie Metcalfe

Sister Abigail Walker thoroughly enjoyed her work in the A&E department, even more so when Dr Ben Taylor arrived! But was Ben the trustworthy and gentle colleague she thought him to be…

BABIES ON HER MIND by Jessica Matthews

Midwife Emily Chandler had not intended to succumb to obstetrician Will Patton. Just because she found herself unexpectedly pregnant was no reason to marry him but Will had other ideas!

OUR NEW MUMMY by Jennifer Taylor
A Country Practice—the second of four books.

Dr David Ross was unprepared for his reaction to the arrival of Laura Mackenzie, consultant paediatrician. Was he betraying the memory of his wife or was it time to move on…

TIME ENOUGH by Carol Wood

Dr Ben Buchan's new locum, Dr Kate Ross, was making a determined effort to start her life again. But did that include becoming involved with the boss?

Available from 4th June 1999

Available at most branches of WH Smith, Tesco, Asda, Martins, Borders, Easons, Volume One/James Thin and most good paperback bookshops

MILLS & BOON®

Makes any time special™

*Bestselling themed romances brought
back to you by popular demand*

Each month By Request brings you three
full-length novels in one beautiful volume
featuring the best of the best.

So if you missed a favourite Romance
the first time around, here is your chance
to relive the magic from some of our
most popular authors.

Look out for
Close Proximity **in May 1999**
**featuring Charlotte Lamb,
Margaret Way and Lindsay Armstrong**

*Available at most branches of WH Smith, Tesco,
Asda, Martins, Borders, Easons,
Volume One/James Thin
and most good paperback bookshops*

FREE!

2 Books
and a surprise gift!

We would like to take this opportunity to thank you for reading this Mills & Boon® book by offering you the chance to take TWO more specially selected titles from the Medical Romance™ series absolutely FREE! We're also making this offer to introduce you to the benefits of the Reader Service™—

- ★ FREE home delivery
- ★ FREE gifts and competitions
- ★ FREE monthly Newsletter
- ★ Books available before they're in the shops
- ★ Exclusive Reader Service discounts

Accepting these FREE books and gift places you under no obligation to buy; you may cancel at any time, even after receiving your free shipment. Simply complete your details below and return the entire page to the address below. *You don't even need a stamp!*

YES! Please send me 2 free Medical Romance books and a surprise gift. I understand that unless you hear from me, I will receive 4 superb new titles every month for just £2.40 each, postage and packing free. I am under no obligation to purchase any books and may cancel my subscription at any time. The free books and gift will be mine to keep in any case.

M9EB

Ms/Mrs/Miss/Mr ....Initials ....

BLOCK CAPITALS PLEASE

Surname...

Address...

....

....Postcode ....

Send this whole page to:
THE READER SERVICE, FREEPOST CN81, CROYDON, CR9 3WZ
(Eire readers please send coupon to: P.O. BOX 4546, DUBLIN 24.)

mps MAILING PREFERENCE SERVICE

(DMA)

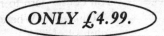